W9-AOU-765

dlrow
eht
yortsed
nac
tac
eht

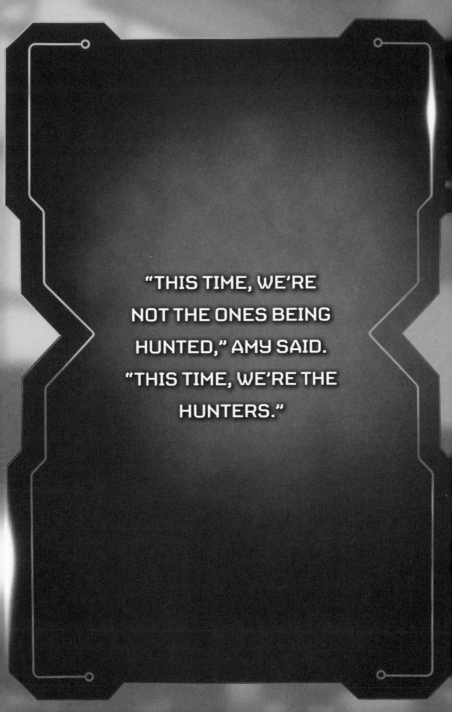

"THIS TIME, WE'RE NOT THE ONES BEING HUNTED," AMY SAID. "THIS TIME, WE'RE THE HUNTERS."

SUPERSPECIAL

OUTBREAK

SUPERSPECIAL

OUTBREAK

THE 39 CLUES

C. ALEXANDER LONDON

SCHOLASTIC INC.

Library of Congress Control Number: 2016943343

ISBN 978-1-338-03705-0

10 9 8 7 6 5 4 3 2 1   16 17 18 19 20

Cover, back cover, and endpapers: © Barry Downard for Scholastic;
31 girl: © Ken Karp for Scholastic; 31 coffee and beach: © neirfy/Fotolia;
48: © Mega Pixel/Shutterstock, Inc.; 67: © Scholastic; 80: © Charice Silverman
for Scholastic; 91: © Russell Kightley/Science Source; 141: © Mega Pixel/
Shutterstock, Inc.; 237: © MSA/Fotolia; 263: © James Levin for Scholastic.

Book and cover design by Charice Silverman

Printed in the U.S.A.   23

First printing 2016

Scholastic US: 557 Broadway • New York, NY 10012
Scholastic Canada: 604 King Street West • Toronto, ON M5V 1E1
Scholastic New Zealand Limited: Private Bag 94407 • Greenmount, Manukau 2141
Scholastic UK Ltd.: Euston House • 24 Eversholt Street • London NW1 1DB

To the Cahill Philippines Clue Hunters,
who sure know how to make a person
feel like part of the family

CHAPTER 1

Boston, Massachusetts

Dan Cahill knew a thing or two about collectors.

When he was younger, he had collected baseball cards, autographs of famous outlaws, Civil War weapons, rare coins, and charcoal rubbings of tombstones. For a while, he had even collected his casts, but he'd broken so many bones that the size and smell of that particular collection had become, to quote his big sister, Amy, "disturbing."

However, the collector he was tracking through the streets of Boston was a different sort of collector entirely. Dan collected stuff he could geek out on—meteor fragments, memorabilia from obscure sports, creepy photos he found at flea markets.

The guy he had his eye on collected stuff he could sell for millions of dollars, stuff that was stolen from archaeology sites around the world and smuggled away from the countries to which it belonged: Buddhist relics from Cambodia, Zoroastrian statues from Iran, religious carvings from Egypt. The artifacts were priceless, sacred, and irreplaceable. They should've been in museums or left in the temples or tombs where they'd been found. They were the sort of things that someone might kill for.

In fact, in this case, someone had. Hundreds of thousands had died because of the artifact this man was carrying in the rolling suitcase currently handcuffed to his wrist, and more might die if he figured out that he was being followed.

But Dan's team was good. The collector didn't have a clue. Dan smiled the smile of a mastermind and wondered if his cousin Jonah Wizard, international pop star, might write him a secret-agent theme song. Dan totally needed a theme song.

"The target went right at Quincy Market," Cara Pierce's voice whispered through Dan's earpiece.

Dan stopped writing lyrics in his imagination and whispered his next orders into the microphone on the cord of his earbuds. "Ham, when he hits Congress Street, execute Operation Bouncing Hammer."

"Gladly," Hamilton Holt replied.

Ham wasn't the most nuanced secret operative in the world, but when something—or *someone*—needed to get knocked down, he was just the guy to do it.

Dan Cahill still looked like your average American teenager. His hair was messy and in need of a cut, his wrinkled T-shirt was an ironic nod to a long-forgotten boy band, but the pen he had tucked behind his ear was actually a CO_2-powered injection syringe loaded with a nauseating toxin perfectly calibrated to the body mass of the smuggler.

Your average American teenager didn't usually have one of those. Although he was just fourteen years old, Dan was the leader of the most powerful family in the world and regularly did things that would make Special Forces soldiers gasp.

Dan glanced up from his phone just as his target appeared at the intersection across from his bench. At the same moment, burly, blond Hamilton Holt, wearing a New England Patriots football jersey and bright blue plastic sunglasses, came barreling out of a gift shop, his fist pumping the air.

"Yeah! Go Pats! Woo!" he yelled, a genuinely enthusiastic cheer for his football team. Never mind that their season hadn't actually started yet. In Boston, no one needed a reason to be loud about their team at any time of year. "We're gonna slay! YE-AHH!"

Ham turned his back to the smuggler to give a double fist pump to the street, and slammed his shoulders into the man as hard as he could.

The smuggler's feet left the ground as he tumbled backward. A smirk flitted across Hamilton's face as the man crashed onto the sidewalk with a sickening thump. The rolling suitcase bounced and wrenched the man's arm but stayed attached.

"I really hope that case is padded on the inside," Amy whispered over the radio.

Dan was already on his feet, rushing to help the guy up.

"Sorry, little man," Ham said to the smuggler on the ground, bending down and yanking the guy to his feet, jostling him as much as possible in the process. "Ya hit tha pahvement *wicked* hahrd."

"Don't try to do an accent," Dan whispered to Ham over the microphone, then spoke to the smuggler on the ground. "I know first aid!" he said cheerily. He grabbed the smuggler by his other arm. He and Ham pulled him in opposite directions. "Careful! He might have a concussion!"

"I'm—I'm fine—" The man tried to shake himself out of Ham's grip, but Ham gripped him tighter. It would leave a bruise. "You are breaking my wrist, you brute!"

"Hey! Aye apahlahgized!" Ham yelled into the smuggler's face. "Why don't ya watch where yah'er goin', ya lubber!"

Ham's Boston accent had turned into a pirate accent, and Dan frowned at him. Ham closed his mouth and squeezed the guy's arm harder. He was a better bruiser than he was an actor.

While the man was focused on freeing himself from Hamilton's vise grip and getting his face away from the large and obviously disturbed teen, Dan pressed the injection pen against the smuggler's backside and fired the needle. At the same instant, Hamilton squeezed the metal of the handcuffs into the smuggler's wrist so hard it made him yelp. "OW!"

The human body can only pay attention to so many sensations at a time, and the pain in his wrist combined with Ham's shouting distracted him completely from the fact he'd just been injected with something. Any soreness he felt, he'd blame on his fall.

Dan stepped back and Ham let the guy go.

The collector turned and nearly knocked Dan over as he rushed past on his way to the door of the restaurant down the street, dragging the suitcase loudly behind him.

Once he'd gone inside, Dan looked over at Hamilton.

"Well done," he said. "You really sold the whole loudmouth fan thing. Except for the pirate bit."

"I never tried an accent before." Ham shrugged. "Thought it'd be fun. But the Pats really *are* gonna slay this year. No one's better than Tom Brady."

Dan agreed, but had more pressing concerns than the coming football season. "Phase one complete. Red Team is clear," he said into his microphone. "Puce Team is a go."

"Affirmative," his sister replied. "But I still don't forgive you for calling us the Puce Team."

"My operation, my team names," Dan said. "Anyway, puce is cool. It's the color of a bruise."

"Puce isn't just a color." Jonah Wizard's voice came over the earpiece. If he was in the right place, he'd be sitting at the best table in the restaurant, his eyes behind dark sunglasses, with a baseball cap pulled low over his face, looking like a celebrity trying to get noticed while trying not to get noticed.

Which was, in fact, exactly what he was.

"*Puce* is the French word for 'flea.' And if the paparazzi find out I was on Team Flea, Imma have Ham give you, Dan, a few puce bruises of your own."

Dan laughed. His cousin Jonah was an international superstar, but no matter how many albums he sold or movie franchises he launched, he couldn't stop worrying about his image. Of course, his image had helped the Cahills out on more missions than they could count, and this one would be no exception. In spite of the potential for embarrassment and/or gruesome death, Jonah never hesitated to do his part for the family.

"Puce Team is a go," Dan repeated into the microphone. He loved saying something was "a go." It was one of his favorite parts of leading a mission. He might start to use it in his everyday life, too. *Breakfast cereal is a go. Sleeping late is a go. Playing six hours of video games is definitely a go.*

"We've got the target inside," Amy said. "Jonah's got a clear view. They put him at a table as far from the bathroom as possible."

"Thank Nellie for that one," said Dan.

"She's not gonna like the next part," Amy replied.

"I think our smuggler will like it even less," Dan answered her. His plan was working perfectly. He never felt more relaxed than when all the pieces came together and everyone did what they were supposed to do. It was like playing chess. And now that the guy was inside the restaurant, it was checkmate time.

Over the earpiece, Amy gasped.

"Oh, come on," said Dan. "Don't be so dramatic. He'll be fine. The poison's just gonna make him puke. I mean . . . a lot. Like, build-an-ark levels of puke . . . but still, it's totally safe."

Amy didn't respond. Not even to call him gross.

Something was wrong. Dan felt the first bead of sweat form at the small of his back.

"All teams check in," he snapped.

"Clear," said Cara.

"Clear," said Ham.

"Clear," said Jonah.

Amy didn't respond.

"Amy?" Dan repeated.

"She's a little busy right now." A man's voice came over the earpiece. "And if any of you do anything to get in my way, I will pull the trigger of the pistol I have pressed to her spine."

CHAPTER 2

Amy felt the barrel of the gun digging into her back and smelled the hot-wing-sauce breath of the man who held it. He spoke over her shoulder so that the microphone on her earpiece could pick up what he was saying, too.

"You will call off your team and leave the target to me," the man said. "No one has to get hurt today. But that case is mine now."

Amy rolled her eyes.

She couldn't believe she had let this hot-sauce-breathed goon sneak up on her. She had insisted on being inside the restaurant to oversee the heist because she figured she had the best chance of being undetected. She knew how to blend in at a fancy restaurant much better than a gawky fourteen-year-old like Dan did. She had argued that she could pass for a college student, and Boston was lousy with college students. It just made more sense.

The real reason she had wanted to be on the inside for this heist was that she knew more about the history of the object in the smuggler's case than any of her cousins and definitely more than her brother. Dan liked making the plan to steal it back from the smuggler, but he didn't care so much about the artifact itself.

Amy had wanted to see it, to hold it, however briefly, before turning it over to the priest who had begged for their help in recovering it.

The suitcase contained a large silver star that had vanished from the Church of the Nativity in Bethlehem in 1847. It had marked the spot where Jesus was said to have been born. At the time, the Church of the Nativity was shared by three different religious communities—Greek Orthodox, Roman Catholic, and Armenian Christians—and when the star was stolen, the priests who shared the church all blamed one another. They fought bitterly, turning the peaceful sanctuary into the site of rowdy brawls. The monks attacked one another with candlesticks and crucifixes, and soldiers were dispatched to back up the different factions.

Then war erupted.

The disappearance of that silver star was one of the sparks that ignited the flame of the Crimean War, a war between the Russian Empire, the Ottoman Empire, Britain, France, and Sardinia that caused over five hundred thousand casualties. It was also the war that made Florence Nightingale, a distant relative of Amy's, famous. She was the founder of modern nursing. Not a bad legacy.

The original silver star that started all the fuss was never recovered. Most thought it gone for good . . . until a distraught priest showed up at the Cahill mansion outside of Boston.

The star had not been lost, it turned out, but hidden for 170 years by an order of monks who feared that revealing it would only cause more arguments. There was enough tension in Bethlehem already, and they didn't want to start another war, this time between nuclear powers.

The star they'd been hiding for all those years had, however, been stolen from them. They couldn't go to the police or Interpol or even the United Nations because they would have to admit that they'd had the star for all that time, and then the arguments over who owned it would begin again. The silver star in the Church of the Nativity had long ago been replaced by a copy, so no one really missed the original. It'd be better if it stayed missing.

The monks came to the Cahills, and they pleaded for help tracking down the thief and stealing the star back before he could sell it on the black market.

Amy had wanted to take the job because of its historical significance.

Dan had wanted to take the job because it sounded like fun.

The rest of the family went along because it was Dan's turn to be in charge. The Cahill family's new system of rotating leadership was working just as it was supposed to, and they'd even found a purpose in solving complex problems for people who had nowhere else to turn. Nellie Gomez, Amy and Dan's legal guardian and now celebrated Boston restaurateur, said they were like the A-Team.

Ham and Jonah argued over which one of them got to be Mr. T, but Dan hadn't gotten the reference to the '80s TV show. Nellie'd told him to Google it sometime.

"Amy, are you okay?" Dan asked over the earpiece.

"Yeah," she said. "The gun barrel's not the most comfortable back massage I've ever felt, and this man's breath is terrible, but he hasn't hurt me."

"I will," the man said. "I know who you are. I know how dangerous you can be, and I won't hesitate to shoot you dead. I want that silver star."

Amy took a deep breath. *What a tiresome goon.*

There might have been a time, long ago, when a man with a gun against her back was a terrifying threat, but that time was long past. Amy had trained and practiced and endured just about every hostage scenario imaginable, and a few that were hardly imaginable at all but had happened to her nonetheless.

She thought through her OODA loop, a fighter-pilot training technique useful in martial arts. It stands for Observe, Orient, Decide, Act. Those simple steps could break down even the fastest, most high-pressure situation into manageable pieces.

So first, she had to observe.

The man was slightly taller than she was and standing with his chest pressed against her back and the gun squeezed in between them. His breath was bad but his hands were steady. He'd used the words "me" and "I," which made Amy think this man was alone.

Big mistake, going up against the Cahills alone.

Next: orient. Where was she exactly?

She and her attacker were in the shadow between two hanging light fixtures in the hallway that led to the restaurant bathrooms. Jonah Wizard couldn't see Amy from where he was sitting, but he had a clear line of sight to the smuggler with the briefcase. Amy could see the smuggler, too. He'd taken a seat at his cramped table farthest from the bathroom. He seemed to be arguing with the host about a better table, but the host, as instructed by owner and head chef Nellie Gomez, was refusing to move him. He still had the suitcase handcuffed to his wrist, standing at the table beside him. His skin was looking greener by the second.

At any moment, he was going to bolt for the bathroom. Dan's plan was gross, but it was working.

Decide: Amy knew what to do. She was going to bring this mission to a close, and quickly.

All she had left to do was act.

The smuggler gagged, raised his hand to his mouth, and stood. He shoved the host out of the way and rushed for the bathroom, dragging his case behind him.

"Puce! Go!" Amy blurted into the microphone.

"Did you say 'puke go' or 'puce go'?" Jonah replied.

"What?" the man with the gun snapped at her.

"Jonah Wizard, now!" Amy yelled, so the whole restaurant turned to look at her.

"Yo! Can I get some peace and quiet up in here?" Jonah shouted, standing and opening his arms in a dramatic pose. The lunchtime crowd in the dim restaurant immediately pulled out their phones and started snapping pictures of the world-famous teen, whose personal net worth was currently estimated somewhere around fifty million dollars.

The flashes were momentarily distracting, and Amy turned sideways, slipping the gun barrel from her back.

The attacker fired a silenced shot into the wall, but Amy had already spun a full one-eighty to face the man. She considered a judo throat chop or a Krav Maga leg sweep, but went with a simpler move instead: a swift knee to his groin.

As the man doubled over in pain, she used her free hand to twist his wrist and force him to drop the pistol.

At that moment, the smuggler rushed into the corridor leading to the bathroom. Amy shoved her attacker into the stumbling smuggler, dropped to one knee, and grabbed the pistol from the carpet.

Her attacker slammed into the smuggler's chest. The smuggler gave him one quick horrified look, and before her attacker could say or do anything, the smuggler hurled all over him.

"Ack!" the man screamed.

"BARF!" The smuggler barfed again, now doubled over and letting loose all over the attacker's shoes.

Gross, but effective. While he was bent over, Amy pressed the barrel of the gun against the chain connecting his suitcase to his wrist.

She fired and with a spark and a snap, the case came free.

She dropped the clip out of the gun, tossed it to the far end of the hall, and bolted for the exit. The smuggler lurched around to grab her, but another heave stopped him short and he fell to the polished concrete floor, face-first in his own sick.

The attacker didn't bother recovering his silenced pistol. He pulled another from an ankle holster and took aim at Amy straight across the restaurant.

Everyone inside screamed and ducked. Only the attacker, Amy, and Jonah Wizard were still standing.

"Freeze and drop the case!" he yelled at Amy.

Amy froze, but she did not drop the case. She turned to face her attacker.

"Who sent you?" she demanded.

"Blahhhhhhhrf," the smuggler on the floor groaned. He tried to stand as he pulled his own gun out of a holster, but he immediately fell again, heaving out something the color of nuclear waste but less appetizing. "Ugggggggh."

"Nobody *sent* me," the man said. "I work for myself. And I am going to make a fortune off that silver star."

"How?" Amy asked. "Everyone thinks it's gone. You won't find anyone to sell it to."

"You can find anything on the Internet," the man said.

"That's your plan?" Amy shook her head. "You're stealing a priceless historical artifact at gunpoint just to try to sell it on the *Internet*?"

The man shrugged and gestured with the barrel of his gun. "Put the case down now and back away."

"You have more guns than brains," said Amy, standing the case up beside her and letting go of the handle.

"But I have more of both than you do," the man said. "Now back away from the case and lie down on the floor."

"BLLLAAAAHFRF," said the smuggler from the floor, tossing his cookies again. The poison Dan had given him really was disgusting. The fact that Ian Kabra had had the recipe memorized was disturbing, too.

"How did you know about our mission?" Amy demanded of the man with the gun. She didn't back away from the case.

The guy didn't seem like a professional thief or a secret agent, so she figured he'd be one of those morons who spills his guts freely when all he really had to do was pull the trigger and walk away. Bad guys, in Amy's experience, all loved to talk.

"I'm a private detective," he told her. "And the priest who hired you, hired me to find you in the first place. How else would some random monk find the most powerful family in the world? Well, once I'd found you and saw all the high-tech stuff you had, I figured there was a big score for me in this. All I had to do was rip off a bunch of teenagers.

I bugged the priest's phone and I waited for you all to make your move."

"Pretty clever," said Amy. "So this is all about making money? You don't care if this thing starts a war?"

The man shrugged again. He had a limited number of gestures, apparently. He was, like most criminals, quite boring. In the end, people driven by greed, anger, or fear were all roughly the same. Amy had found that it was only love, loyalty, and heroism that came in infinite varieties.

And at that moment, one of the most loving, loyal, and heroic people Amy knew was making her move.

Nellie Gomez, Dan and Amy's former nanny, guardian, and protector, stepped from the kitchen. Amy felt bad that Nellie's brand-new restaurant would need to hire professional cleaners to mop up all the smuggler's puke.

Nellie raised her gleaming Yoshihiro Mizu Yaki Honyaki chef's knife in the air. It was a custom-made, five-thousand-dollar precision blade imported from Japan. Amy and Dan had given it to her to celebrate her restaurant's grand opening earlier that summer. Now she hurled the knife through the air. It sliced straight into the gun barrel with such force that it snagged the weapon right out of the man's hand and pinned it to the far wall just beside a tasteful modern painting Jonah had donated.

"Wow." Nellie marveled at her own throw. "You weren't lying, kiddo! That thing can cut steel!"

"Ah!" the man screamed and charged for the gun. Unfortunately for him, he slipped and fell in the smuggler's puke and smacked his teeth on the floor, grunting in pain just as the sirens wailed on the street outside.

"So, uh, Amy? Boston PD is here," Dan told her over the earpiece. "You might want to grab the case and go. Jonah? Can you handle things at the restaurant?"

"I got you covered, cuz," said Jonah. "Boston PD loves me ever since I did that 'stay in school' TV spot for them. Team Puce needs no excuse, we fresh like juice and on the loose!"

"Seriously?" Ham's voice groaned in all their earpieces. "Were you thinking of that this whole time?"

"I had to do something while I waited for Amy and Nellie to take care of that loser," Jonah said. "Figured I'd lay down some rhymes."

"All right," Dan said. "We'll let the cops mop those two up and Jonah will cover our tracks. Everybody else, fall out."

As Amy left the restaurant with the case, she mouthed a thank-you to Nellie, who bowed gracefully and crossed the restaurant to remove her knife from the gun and the wall. Amy trusted her to handle all the witnesses, too. She'd be giving out free dinners for months, but no one would say anything to the cops or the press that Nellie didn't want said. Her food was that good.

It'd been a messy mission, but a successful one.

The only downside would be her little brother's gloating.

Dan would, of course, take full credit for the mission, as if his puke plot, and not Amy's quick martial arts or Nellie's blade skills, was the real reason they'd pulled it off.

Either way, the silver star of Bethlehem would safely disappear once again, and Amy was feeling pretty good about it.

Priceless artifact saved, bad guys arrested, and World War III prevented.

All in a day's work for the Cahill kids.

CHAPTER 3

Agent Gimler and Agent Pratt—it didn't matter which was which—sat side by side in their dark sedan and watched the Cahill siblings stroll past the arriving police cars. The kids walked calmly, like they didn't have a care in the world or any idea that the massive SWAT team surging toward the swanky restaurant, Grace's Table, had anything to do with them.

The boy, Dan Cahill, age fourteen, put a finger to his ear, listening.

"Turn up the volume," said Agent Gimler.

"It's as loud as it will go," said Agent Pratt.

All they heard were two static clicks. They'd been monitoring the frequency all day, and they'd heard every part of the plan unfold. They'd been tempted to swoop in, guns drawn, when the rogue private detective started shooting, but they'd restrained themselves. It was hard to sit back and watch a bunch of teenagers in mortal danger without helping, but they had to see how these kids would react when their plans fell apart.

Agent Gimler and Agent Pratt were impressed.

"Two clicks," said Agent Pratt.

"A signal, I'm sure," said Agent Gimler.

Agent Pratt whistled, impressed again. "They know the police will be on every frequency in the area in case this restaurant incident is part of a terrorist attack."

"So they've gone quiet," said Agent Gimler, nodding. "I'm convinced. They're our team."

"Agreed," said Agent Pratt.

They pulled the car from its spot and followed the kids from a distance, driving past and circling back. They didn't need to stay too close. They had a tracking device on the Cahill vehicle, an inconspicuous minivan. No one would bat an eye when a bunch of kids got into the back of a minivan in historic Boston. School trips, church groups, summer camp outings—kids in vans were the norm. The Cahills had considered every detail.

The driver was the big blond one, Hamilton Holt, eighteen years old. He'd changed out of his Patriots jersey and was dressed like an Abercrombie & Fitch model, which blended in perfectly with all the college kids in the area. In the front passenger seat sat Cara Pierce, her hair dyed black. She was the estranged daughter of J. Rutherford Pierce, former presidential candidate. An expert computer hacker. Agents Gimler and Pratt had a thick file on her.

They followed the van as it wove its way through the labyrinth of Boston's streets. At one point they lost it, due to Hamilton's habitual evasive maneuvers, and had to find it again on their route back to the Cahill mansion in Attleboro.

Eighteen-year-old Ian Kabra, British national and former leader of the family, had been waiting at the home with the old priest from Bethlehem. When they arrived, the fellow took the suitcase from them, kissed them each on each cheek, which made Kabra roll his eyes and Dan wince, and then went on his way.

"He didn't pay them," said Agent Gimler.

"They did the job for free?" said Agent Pratt.

"Maybe this will be easier than we thought," replied Agent Gimler.

Once Jonah Wizard arrived, having sorted out the mess in Nellie Gomez's restaurant, the agents eased the car forward and approached the front gates of the house. The mansion was an impressive reconstruction of a historic nineteenth-century home. The high-tech security was, however, very twenty-first century.

"Who is it?" Cara Pierce's voice came over the intercom that was hidden inside a thicket of thorny roses growing around the gate. The agents knew they were being watched, probably from multiple cameras.

"Agent Gimler," said Agent Gimler.

"And Agent Pratt," said Agent Pratt. "We're with the government."

"You'll have to be more specific," she replied.

"The *US* government," Agent Gimler said.

Without bothering to take her finger off the intercom, Cara Pierce called to the others. "Hey, guys, it's those spies who've been following us for weeks. Should I let them in?"

Agent Gimler raised an eyebrow at Agent Pratt. "This is definitely the team we need."

The gate swung open and they eased their car up the driveway toward the grand mansion inhabited by a motley crew of the world's most powerful teenagers.

They were, at this moment, also the world's best hope for survival.

CHAPTER 4

Attleboro, Massachusetts

Saladin the cat, a pampered Egyptian Mau, perched on a reproduction seventeenth-century end table that he apparently believed was his personal cat condo.

This particular piece had delicate tulipwood scrollwork and intricate satinwood inlays, and Saladin groomed himself upon it with great disdain. The cat would never have treated a real antique this way, but he was a feline with exceptional taste, and a reproduction seventeenth-century end table, no matter how finely crafted, did not earn the respect he had given to the original, which had been lost in a fire.

Ian respected the cat's contempt and did not bother to move him as the agents sat down on the reproduction Louis XIV sofa opposite him.

"My cousins will be along shortly," Ian said to them, passing his eyes over their dark suits, noting the bulge in the shoulders where their concealed firearms caused their jackets to bunch. The suits were not well tailored and reeked, to Ian's mind, of government salaries. "Might I ask with which government agency you gentlemen are affiliated?"

The agents looked at each other, then back at Ian, and spoke at the same time.

"The Department of Agriculture," said one.

"Fish and Wildlife Service," said the other.

Agent Gimler glared at Agent Pratt and frowned. *So they are CIA.*

That explained the cheap suits. Ian much preferred the fashion sense of the British secret service, MI6, who had the good taste to model their own fashion choices off their most famous fictional counterpart, James Bond. An MI6 man got his suits custom-tailored on Savile Row, just as Ian himself did. These American operatives probably got theirs from a place called Bubba's Suit Barn.

Ian sighed loudly, demonstrating to them his utter contempt. He wanted them unsure of themselves, slightly nervous. He'd found people were more honest when they were not completely confident. Now that Ian wasn't in charge of the Cahill family's vast global network of business leaders, inventors, artists, spies, and accountants (the underappreciated magicians of modern finance), he had regained his customary confidence. He could focus on the things that interested him, rather than what interested every other Cahill. Leave those worries to Dan and Amy.

Right now, he was interested in getting a new suit, something with burgundy accents for autumn. He'd book a ticket to London this afternoon, as soon as they dispensed with these Central Intelligence Agency buffoons.

He watched them in silence, letting Saladin's loud grooming fill the space between them. The agents shifted uncomfortably until the grand wooden doors to the library swept open and the rest of the family thundered in.

When they were all together, Ian couldn't help but think of them like a crash of rhinoceroses. Lovable rhinoceroses, to be sure, but still, loud and boorish and utterly American.

Dan took the chair closest to the two agents and folded one leg up under himself, looking every bit the boy that he was. Ian straightened his back to project a slightly more authoritative posture, even though, at present, Dan was the leader of the Cahill family. Amy sat on the couch beside Ian, resting her hands sensibly in her lap, and Cara perched on the armrest at his other side, her hand resting on his back. This caused him to sit up even straighter.

Jonah strutted around behind the couch and struck a pose against the mantel of the fireplace.

Hamilton was the last to enter, and he shut the door behind him. He stayed standing, using his considerable size to loom behind the two agents, arms crossed in front of him and a scowl impressively etched across his face. This was his *bodyguard* face, which he used to great effect as Jonah's personal security detail. The rainbow bracelet he'd taken to wearing undercut his authority somewhat, but Ham appeared to enjoy flattening anyone who made a less than supportive comment about it.

Everyone was in position, like a family portrait, posed and poised, which had the further effect of confusing the CIA agents.

This was not accidental.

Best to keep these guys on edge. Dan had learned the strategy from Ian himself.

"So, farm boys," Dan addressed them, using some kind of American slang for CIA agents that Ian was certain Dan had picked up from watching Hollywood action movies. Dan modeled so much of his leadership style on Hollywood action movies, Ian marveled that he hadn't accidentally caused Armageddon. "What do you want?" Dan asked. *With all the grace and aplomb of a wild boar.*

"We won't waste your time," said Agent Pratt. "We know you've had a long day."

"You know that, huh?" Dan drummed his fingers on the arm of his chair. He had an insouciant and carefree manner that Ian usually found most disagreeable, but he did enjoy how confused it was making these CIA agents. They were very unsure how they should talk to a fourteen-year-old with as much power as Dan wielded.

"They've been following us for two weeks," Cara reminded him.

"Oh right," said Dan. "So you know we just, like, prevented World War Three over a silver star, right? You're welcome."

Agent Gimler cleared his throat. "Yes, it was a very impressive operation, but the job we have for you will demand a great deal more . . ." The agent glanced around the room, searching for a word.

"Finesse?" Ian suggested.

"Yes," Agent Gimler replied, with a respectful nod. "Finesse."

"So no puking?" Dan added. "What's the point of beating the bad guys of the world if you can't make them toss their cookies while you're at it?"

"I'm sorry to say," Amy cut in, "we don't work for the government. *Any* government. Even our own."

"Yeah," said Dan. "We take the jobs we decide are worthy. If you have a problem, if no one else can help, and if you can find us, then maybe you can hire the Cahills."

"We have money to pay you—" Agent Pratt began, then cocked his head at Dan. "Wait. Was that the A-Team motto?"

Dan grinned. "Yeah," he said. "I Googled it. Anyway, you can't actually hire us. Check out the room you're in. We don't need your money. That cat—" He pointed at Saladin, who stopped grooming himself when all eyes turned to him.

"*Mrrrp*," said the cat.

"That cat's lunch costs more than most government salaries," Dan said. "We can't even spend all the money we already have. In fact, it should be *us* offering *you* money, just to get rid of some of it. Want some money?"

"Dan!" Amy interrupted her brother. "You made your point. Also, you just offered to bribe two government officials."

"Oh, right. Sorry." Dan pulled his leg out from under him and leaned forward to talk quietly to the agents. "The point is, our services are not for sale, and if they were, the US government couldn't afford them."

Ian cleared his throat loudly. It was terribly uncouth to boast about one's wealth, even if Dan was technically correct. As the leaders of the Cahill family, they had access to a network of bank accounts and investments worth billions.

Agent Gimler looked at Agent Pratt, then nodded. Agent Pratt reached into his briefcase and pulled out a folder, which he opened and studied for a moment. "Perhaps this will change your mind," he said. "One of your cousins is in serious trouble."

Hamilton was the only one at an angle to see the contents of the folder at first, and his eyebrows snapped up in surprise. When the agent turned it around for everyone else to see, Ian felt his heart turn to a hot coal of rage in his chest. Amy took in a quick breath, and, Ian noticed, Dan dug his fingers into the armrest of his chair deep enough to mar the upholstery.

The picture was of a traitor.

In a surveillance photo sat Sinead Starling, their estranged cousin, her red hair falling over her shoulders and her usual polo shirt as crisp and tidy

Ext cam 3

as ever. She was at an outdoor café, somewhere tropical.

"The man she is talking to across the table is a retired military virologist named Dr. Donald Miller," said Agent Pratt. "Dr. Miller was renowned for his work on biological weapons, before he defected to Cuba."

"Sinead is her own person," said Amy, forcing a casualness into her voice Ian knew she didn't feel. "She can talk to whomever she likes."

"Be that as it may," said Agent Gimler, "shortly after this meeting, we lost track of her. And shortly after *that*, we lost a very large supply of genetically modified goat pox virus."

"That doesn't sound so bad," said Amy. "Goat pox only infects goats. It's not zoonotic."

Dan gave Amy one of his puzzled looks, showing a lack of knowledge that Ian would never dream of revealing to someone else. When he didn't know something, Ian just smiled and nodded and then looked it up later. For example, he also had no idea what *zoonotic* meant, but he wasn't about to admit that in front of anyone.

"Zoonosis," Amy said with an exasperated look at Dan, "is the transmission of diseases between species. It's how most new diseases appear. They're carried by animal hosts, sometimes harmlessly, but they can mutate to infect humans or the other way around. So, like, Saladin here can snuggle with you when you get the flu, because human influenza virus doesn't affect cats, and you can snuggle with him when he gets the flu, because cat flu is not zoonotic. It doesn't affect humans. But if you had a bird with the bird flu, that one is zoonotic and could infect you."

"But goat pox can't?" Hamilton asked.

"Correct," Amy confirmed.

"Why do you know so much about goat diseases?" Dan asked his sister, the very question that Ian himself had been wondering.

"Remember when I wanted to be a veterinarian?" she replied.

Dan nodded.

Ian could imagine Amy being a wonderful veterinarian, except she was also a wonderful covert operative. She could nurse a wounded squirrel back to health or deliver a brutal roundhouse kick. He was glad about the path she had chosen. He liked her much more as a soldier of fortune.

"That's correct. Goat pox doesn't pose a threat to humans. Until you change its genetic structure," Agent Pratt corrected her.

"Pox viruses have killed hundreds of millions of people in history. Who on earth would be daft enough to mess with the genetic structure of a disease like that?" Ian asked, as the pale faces of the agents in front of him went very still. "Oh." He slapped his own knees. "You Americans would. I should have guessed."

"What did you do?" Amy demanded.

"That information is classified," said Agent Gimler.

"We need you to locate your cousin, Sinead Starling," said Agent Pratt, "and recover these virus samples before they unleash a health crisis of unimaginable devastation."

"And you'd like to avoid having the US government's secret goat pox experiments in the headlines, too, I presume?" Ian suggested.

The agents nodded.

"Typical," he grunted.

"Why do you think Sinead is the one who took your virus samples?" Hamilton leaned over the two men on the couch, causing them to tense. "She might have nothing to do with it."

Hamilton had always had a soft spot for Sinead, even after she became a traitor to the family. But Ian's sister might still be alive if it weren't for Sinead, so he wasn't quite as ready to forgive.

"We don't *think* Sinead's involved in our missing goat pox," said Agent Pratt. "We know it."

He pulled another picture from his file. It was Sinead again, this time on a security camera, all in black. Ian's jaw clenched. He wanted to snatch the picture from them and shout at it, but that would have been rather undignified.

"She broke into the containment storage freezers at USAMRIID," Agent Gimler said.

"*USAMRIID* stands for United States Army Medical Research Institute of Infectious Diseases," Cara explained before anyone asked. Again, Ian was grateful. He'd had no idea. "It's the US Army's center for research into the defense against biological warfare."

How does she know this off the top of her head?

Cara met his eyes and shrugged. "I run threat assessment models on my computer in my spare time," she told him. "USAMRIID is a prime national security target."

"You're a remarkable person," Ian told her, and took her hand in his.

He ignored Dan's groan from the other side of the coffee table.

"We have Sinead on camera stealing the virus samples from the Biosafety Level Four containment lab," Agent Gimler continued.

"That's the most secure level," Jonah cut in. "Scientists wear pressurized suits with breathing hoses and have to take decontamination showers to avoid even a molecule of the stuff in there escaping."

This time, Ian and Cara looked at Jonah with surprise.

"What?" He shrugged. "You don't remember my single 'Contagious Love'? I played a love doctor in the video, but a tear in my suit got me infected with romance and rhythm."

"I saw that video!" Agent Pratt cracked a smile for the first time since he'd arrived.

"Everyone saw that video," Jonah told him. "It got nine hundred eighty-seven million views."

"We can assume the consequences of a release of Dr. Miller's modified goat pox would *not* be as much fun," Agent Gimler cut in.

Agent Pratt leaned forward. "I assure you, you want us to find Sinead Starling before this virus gets out."

"No," said Dan, standing to signal that their meeting was over. "You want *us* to find her before this virus gets out."

Ian didn't like to express differences of opinion in front of outsiders. He tried to give Dan a warning, but Dan had that *I'm about to make an impulsive Dan Cahill decision* look on his face, and there was little chance of stopping him. This was the problem with rotating the leadership of the Cahill family among them. They were currently being led by a fourteen-year-old with a superhero complex.

"We'll take the job," said Dan, sticking his hand out for a shake.

"But when we find Sinead, *we* decide what happens to her. She's one of ours, after all," Amy added.

"Was!" corrected Dan and Ian at the exact same time.

Dan turned back to the CIA agents. "She *was* one of ours. She's not anymore."

On that, Ian and Dan were in full agreement.

"I'm sure there is a fascinating story of friendship and betrayal there," said Agent Pratt. "But it's none of our concern. Take it up with her when you find her. Preferably before she unleashes the virus on the world."

"Sinead wouldn't do that," Hamilton said. "I'm sure she stole the virus for a good reason."

The two CIA agents stood and stepped up to him in front of the door. For a moment, it looked like Ham was about to hit them, which Ian would have enjoyed seeing, but which would not have been very useful to their current situation.

"We really don't care about her reasons," Agent Gimler said. "We care about getting the virus back under lock and key. If it is released into the world . . . well . . . maybe you should ask Dr. Miller what horror might unfold. If you can find him, that is. He hasn't been seen since that fateful meeting with your dear Sinead Starling."

CHAPTER 5

The CIA agents showed themselves out. Amy looked at the stunned faces of everyone left in the library. The silence sat heavily on the room.

The only sounds came from Saladin, purring because he had found the perfect patch of sunlight. That patch of sunlight happened to be on Ian's lap, and his sour-lemon expression told everyone just how he felt about the cat sunbathing across his pants.

"We should put him in his crate when company is present," Ian said. "Outsiders will think we're soft if the cat is seen to have free rein over our headquarters."

"Saladin *does* have free rein, though," said Dan. "And he escapes whenever we put him in his crate anyway. It wouldn't do any good."

Amy stood up to leave Ian and Saladin on the couch. She wanted another look at the photos the CIA agents had left behind.

"Sinead Starling," she said aloud. She hadn't spoken Sinead's name in a long time. The girl had been her best friend. They had trusted her; Amy had trusted her the most. And then she had betrayed them all and nearly killed Amy in the process.

Amy had forgiven her, but it was easy to forgive someone when you never had to think about them. What Sinead had done those years ago, she had done to save her brothers, Ted and Ned, who'd been seriously injured in the Clue hunt, and Amy could understand that. She had wondered at the time how far she herself would go to help Dan.

"This might be a new low, even for her," Ian said.

"Come on, we don't know that Sinead's guilty of anything here," said Ham. His family had been the ones that injured Sinead's brothers. Forgiving her was his way of making himself forgivable.

Poor Ham. Guilt wasn't a pain you could power through like wind sprints.

"She strangled Amy and tried to shoot her," Dan reminded Ham, shaking his head. "She's a cold-blooded, redheaded reptile." Dan's tone of voice could have curdled milk. Even Saladin looked up from his grooming in alarm.

"But she saved Amy's life later," said Ham. "She's not *all* bad."

"Be real," Jonah addressed his best friend. "Sinead stole an experimental disease from a government lab. That's not exactly *good*."

"Sure, okay," said Ham. "But what was the government doing with that experimental disease? I mean, that's not exactly *good*, either. Maybe she was stealing it to keep it safe? Maybe she was stealing it to hide it *from* the very people those CIA guys think she's stealing it *for*?"

"That is very imaginative," Ian scoffed. "And also complete fairy-tale nonsense."

"Who are you calling a fairy, Brit-fuff-fuff?" Ham rounded the couch, fists balled to knock Ian out.

"Hey!" Amy put herself between Hamilton and Ian. Sinead Starling wasn't even in the room and she was tearing them all apart.

"It's great you're such an optimist, Ham," she told him. "And I honestly don't know what Sinead is up to," she told Ian. "We won't know until we find her, so *that* is what we should focus on. She can tell her side of the story herself. The important thing now is locating Sinead and securing that virus." She looked at her brother. Appealing to Dan's mastermind side might keep his wrathful side in check. "We took the job, so let's do the job right."

Dan agreed.

"You guys think Sinead Starling's devious, right?" Cara asked. She was the only one who hadn't known Sinead.

"Yes," said Amy. "She infiltrated our family, pretended to be on our side, but was really spying the whole time. She tried to frame Ian and, well . . ."

"She nearly killed Amy," Dan added again. "So yeah, you could say she's devious."

"She tricked all of you?" Cara asked. "Even Ian, who is not easily fooled—" Amy noticed Ian puff up his chest a little at this, until Saladin hissed and made him go back to the position he'd been in before. "She did all of this, but here, robbing a top-secret government lab, she doesn't wear a mask? Did she not think there would be cameras?"

"She *wanted* us to see her," Amy said.

Cara nodded.

It was an interesting theory. It meant she wanted the rest of the Cahills to know what she was up to.

But *why*?

What *was* she up to?

"I think we need to know more about this pox virus," said Amy. "And about why Sinead would want it."

"I'm on it," said Cara, pulling up information from the Centers for Disease Control on her phone. "'Smallpox is a serious and often fatal airborne infectious disease,'" she read.

She spun the phone around to show a picture of a human victim of smallpox, their skin waxy and tight with angry raised bumps all over it.

"That's gross," said Dan.

"Says the Vomit Mastermind," Amy scoffed, but took the phone from Cara to research more. "In history, smallpox is believed to have killed over three hundred million people, including Ramses the Fifth in ancient Egypt, Louis the Fifteenth in eighteenth-century France, and even one of Benjamin Franklin's son's. Abraham Lincoln had smallpox but survived. So did Queen Elizabeth the First."

"There is no cure for smallpox, but a massive vaccination campaign in the twentieth century eradicated the disease," Cara went on. "The last naturally occurring case of smallpox appeared in 1977 in Somalia, although samples of the disease exist in laboratories around the world, including samples suspected to be held by rogue nations."

"I can confirm this is the case," said Ian.

Amy raised an eyebrow at him.

"The Lucian branch of the family had extensive contacts in what you might call *rogue nations*," he said. "But I assure you, the stockpiles are secure."

Dan also raised an eyebrow at him.

"Don't give me that look!" Ian objected. "Lucians have kept the world in balance for a long time. The fact that some of the madmen who run these countries haven't blown us all to bits is thanks, in part, to the Lucian branch of the family. You're welcome, by the way."

"My thank-you note must have gotten lost in the mail," Dan replied sarcastically.

"Okay, so that's smallpox," said Jonah, changing the subject. "But Sinead didn't steal smallpox. She stole some kind of genetically modified goat pox!"

"Just about every species on earth has its own pox viruses, and they mostly only affect that species," Amy explained, much more comfortable providing the facts than managing everyone's feelings. "There is camel pox and caterpillar pox. Cat pox"—for a moment it looked like Saladin understood and was alarmed, but he merely had a

hairball, which he delicately spat onto Ian's pants—
"monkey pox, chicken pox—"

"Humans get that one," Dan said. "I had it when I was little. It itched like crazy. I had to take a bath in oatmeal."

"But afterward you were immune to it, right?" Amy said. "You couldn't get it again. That's how vaccines work. Exposure to a form of the disease produces antibodies in the blood that make a person immune. The smallpox vaccine was developed hundreds of years ago from cow pox, by a man named Edward Jenner."

"By a *British man* named Edward Jenner," Ian interjected. "If we are going to discuss contributions to science, I would like it to be remembered that this pox vaccine was discovered by *my* people, while yours are the ones building secret virus laboratories."

"Yeah, God save the Queen." Dan rolled his eyes. "So he developed a smallpox vaccine. But, if every species has its own pox, then that vaccine wouldn't work on, say, goat pox?"

"Right," said Cara. She brought up another photo. It was a picture of a field covered in fur. For a moment Amy didn't know what she was looking at, and then it made sense. Dead goats. Thousands and thousands of dead goats.

"Oh man." Dan sat back into his chair.

Amy understood all too well what had made her brother slump. "If that lab was doing experiments to alter the genes of goat pox so that it could infect humans—?"

"We'd be defenseless against it," said Ian. "No immunity. No known vaccine would work. No known cure."

"And any contact with the infected spreads the infections," Cara said. "Poxes are some of the most contagious diseases on Earth. Breathing in even the tiniest particle can be enough to spread the virus." She flipped to another picture. Another herd of dead goats. And another. And another.

Amy's stomach felt woozy. "When smallpox killed three hundred million people, it was before the age of easy air travel and high population megacities. A disease like that now could spread like a wildfire. One sneeze in an airport, and billions of people—"

"Dead as goats," said Dan.

"Why on earth would Sinead want samples of a disease like *that*?" Ham gripped the back of the sofa so hard, he cracked the wood.

"She's not looking so innocent now, is she?" Dan asked Ham.

Ham shook his head. The back of the couch tore off. "Oops."

"We can't let ourselves get distracted by questions of Sinead's guilt or her innocence," Amy said. "Making assumptions will cloud our judgment. All we know for a *fact* is that she met with this Dr. Miller and then she stole this modified goat pox virus from a government lab. We don't know what the modifications to it actually are, but we think she *wanted* us to know she stole it."

"But we don't know why," said Jonah.

"She could be luring us into a trap," suggested Ian.

"Like Amy said," Dan cut in. "We can't assume anything. All we can do is find her before something terrible happens."

"So, *mastermind*, do you have a plan?" Ian asked.

Amy looked to Dan, too. He had the natural cunning of a Cahill leader, more than she did, and his plans—though often involving gross bodily functions—were usually ingenious.

His tongue poked from the corner of his mouth as he thought, then he cracked a wide smile. "Of course I have a plan," he said at last. "We're gonna clip this Starling's wings."

"Uh, Dan." Amy put her hand on her brother's shoulder. "That's not really a plan. That's more like a catchphrase."

"Whatever." Dan shrugged. "It sounded cool, didn't it?"

Amy sighed. Whenever Dan started coming up with catchphrases, something very dangerous was about to happen.

CHAPTER 6

Havana, Cuba

She was being followed. These days, she was always being followed.

There was never a moment when the guards weren't watching her. Even when she broke into the containment lab at USAMRIID, they were watching her, making sure she did as ordered.

Sinead Starling always did as ordered.

She wanted this part of the mission to succeed, but not for the reasons that they thought. If there was one thing Sinead knew how to do, it was to keep her reasons to herself.

She had taken the virus samples and smuggled them out of the country, just like they had wanted her to do. She'd brought the samples to Havana, hidden inside her makeup case.

And then she'd had second thoughts. She began to doubt.

But her employers didn't care about her doubts. They'd put her in motion and they told her it was too late to back out. They attached bodyguards to her with clear instructions: If Sinead Starling tries to change the plan, they were to kill her on the spot.

If they killed her, their plan would still proceed. *That's why I have to keep going,* she told herself. *If I don't do this, someone else will. Someone even more dangerous than me. I started all this, so I have to be the one to see it through.*

She knew she was lying to herself, though.

The real reason she kept going was simple: She was afraid. Sinead Starling did not want to die.

So she strolled along the wide seaside promenade in Havana called the Malecón, and she took in the beautiful sights. To her left, decaying buildings lined the road, their lights twinkling on and off as power came and went. The windows glowed yellow against the pink and blue stucco facades. She walked the wide sidewalk opposite the buildings along the waist-high wall that held back the ocean. The Caribbean lapped midnight blue against its edge, and the stars burned above.

The saltwater air tickled her nose and she looked from the promenade across the sea ninety miles to Florida. She imagined she could see cars zipping up Route 1, which began in Key West at the lowest point of the continental United States and ran straight up the East Coast all the way to Maine. On its way, it passed right through Attleboro, Massachusetts.

She missed her one-time home. She missed having friends.

Her brothers, Ted and Ned, were her life, but every time she looked at them, she was reminded of the horrible things she'd done on their behalf. How she had betrayed everyone she cared about, and how all she'd done was cause disaster. Ted was still blind and Ned still suffered debilitating headaches. She hadn't helped them at all. But she had tried to murder Amy. She had tried to frame Ian. She had done horrible things; she knew that. She wanted, more than anything, to be forgiven.

Her brothers both said, so sweetly, that they didn't blame her for what she had done. But she could tell they were a little afraid of her. Now that they knew what she was capable of, they could never fully trust her again.

But this plan—*her plan*—this would be her redemption.

She wondered what Amy and Dan were up to at this very moment in Attleboro. Had they heard what she had done yet? Had they seen her face in the surveillance photos? Were they starting to work up that old Cahill heroism to come after her?

She hoped so.

She needed them. She needed them to see what she could do. Sinead was going to save the world.

But first she had to risk destroying it.

Sinead took a deep breath and walked to the edge of the seawall, resting her palms on the warm concrete. The Malecón was known as Havana's front porch. Not a lot of people had air-conditioning in their homes, and Havana was a hot Caribbean city, so all the young people left their sweltering apartments and came to the promenade to breathe the fresh air off the ocean. All around her, young people laughed and joked and danced and kissed.

Sinead, being young herself, blended in perfectly, except for her bright red hair. She'd put on a light flowing sundress and wrapped a light silk shawl around her shoulders to cover her pale freckled skin. No one paid her any attention at all as she turned her back to the ocean. No one looked askance as she stretched her limbs and smiled at a group of teenagers who'd formed a drum circle beside her.

She decided to dance, grooving and swaying to the rhythm. By dancing, she disappeared, even to the operatives who were following her. She looked like just another teenager out for a night of fun.

Except one of her hands crept into her shoulder bag and slipped out a small glass vial.

As she danced she let the vial slide down her leg, hitting the ground with the tiniest of clanks. Then she raised her foot, just another dance move, following the rhythm of the drums.

She covered her nose and mouth with the silk shawl, held her breath, and stomped down.

The glass vial shattered, and she quickly danced away from it, grooving and moving like a girl caught up in the music.

It wasn't until she was three blocks away that she breathed again.

Her heart still beat like the drums she could no longer hear.

She'd done it.

There was no turning back now.

The operatives sidled up to her, matching her pace and escorting her into the dark side streets of the Vedado neighborhood. No one was out and the streetlights weren't working. Old pastel mansions with high colonnades looked abandoned all around, except she could hear the crying of children inside, the sound of radios and televisions, laughter and music. There was life in all the darkness.

No one had any idea that at that very moment, with every breath, the dancers on the Malecón sucked in tiny particles of a brand-new virus. Microscopic cells were attaching to the insides of their lungs, sliding into their bloodstreams, multiplying, growing. With every breath, with every heartbeat, the little particles spread.

When they'd spread enough, the symptoms would start. And the panic, the terror.

The city would be paralyzed. It would need a savior.

And Sinead would save it.

A vintage black-and-white 1957 Oldsmobile cruised toward them. She climbed in before her bodyguards, and once they started rolling, she spoke to the man in front.

"It's done," she said.

"Good," said the man, clearing his throat. The throat clearing was a habit of his, and the sound of it had started to drive Sinead crazy. After months working at his side, she felt like she would scream if she had to hear him clear his throat one more time.

He cleared his throat one more time.

She didn't scream. She had to control herself. She couldn't risk being cut out of the plan. She couldn't raise his suspicions. "Mr. West, when do you think they will begin to show symptoms?" she asked instead. She made sure to call him *mister*, not *doctor*. She liked to remind him that he wasn't a doctor.

"By tomorrow evening," he told her. "It takes at least a day to grow to effective levels."

"And how will we know?"

"We'll have agents watching every hospital," Mr. West said. "The symptoms are unique. We'll know very quickly if the infection worked."

"And then we'll give them the cure?"

He nodded, but she knew he wasn't telling the truth. Jonathan West did not get to be the Director of Special Products for ShkrellX Pharmaceuticals by giving away medicine for free. He wasn't a doctor or a scientist, but he knew how to make money.

"What do we do if the cure doesn't work?" Sinead asked.

"It's too late to call off the plan," Mr. West told her. "The clock is already ticking and billions could be lost."

Sinead's mouth went dry. She found herself clearing her own throat, just to get the next question out. "Do you really think billions of people will die?"

"Who knows?" He shrugged and cleared his throat again. "But I was talking about dollars."

CHAPTER 7

Attleboro, Massachusetts

Thinking about Sinead made Dan's head get hot and his teeth grind against each other. This was the curse of having a perfect memory. Yeah, he could count cards in blackjack, recite the starting batting order for every baseball World Series since 1947, and fill in the street names on a blank map of any major city in the world, but he could also never forget a betrayal.

He still remembered exactly what Sinead had looked like when she tried to shoot Amy.

Memory wasn't good for forgiveness.

"I knew Berkeley, England, sounded familiar!" Amy declared, reading, like she always did, from one the mansion's thick leather-bound books. Why she always turned to books instead of the Internet was a mystery to Dan, but he'd learned to respect his sister's methods over the years, however boring they were. This book was a big medical encyclopedia with onion-skin-thin pages and tiny type. There were black-and-white line drawings of diseases and wounds scattered throughout, like a picture book designed to give small children nightmares. "Berkeley was the home of Edward Jenner, the man who discovered the smallpox vaccine!"

"And that's where the Starlings moved after Singapore? Coincidence, perhaps?" Ian suggested. "You understand that, unlike America, England is very old. There isn't a little town anywhere in the British Isles that doesn't have some historical significance. There is literally no town Sinead could have moved to where something momentous did not occur."

"Calm down there, Prime Minister," Dan ribbed. He loved making the Brit-fuff-fuff's blood pressure rise. "You and Ham and Jonah will just pop in and make *sure* it's a coincidence."

"I should go, too," said Cara, with a glance at Ian.

"Ew! I am not sending you on a romantic getaway!" Dan declared. "If I send you with Ian, then Ham will want to bring his boyfriend and Jonah will want to bring one of his little groupies, and pretty soon the whole mission will be forgotten while you guys canoodle with your crushes in the English countryside!"

"I do *not* canoodle!" Ian objected.

"I'm not dating anybody right now," Ham complained.

"And I don't hang out with groupies. I hang out with models. Read the papers."

"We know you do," said Dan, and everyone in the room snickered.

Jonah wasn't lying, but what the tabloids didn't know was that the models he hung out with were model trains. In the last few months, Jonah Wizard had become an amateur model train enthusiast and turned an entire floor of his eight-thousand-square-foot Los Angeles mansion into a miniature hand-painted train garden. He'd even built a perfectly accurate model of the Attleboro mansion, with a tiny little Saladin cat figure in the window that purred every time the train passed. He'd named the train the Wizard Express.

"I don't want to go on this mission because of Ian," Cara said. "I want to go because Edward Jenner was an Ekat and you might want an Ekat along."

"Oh, right," Dan said. He had an amazing memory for stuff he cared about, but he rarely paid attention to where everyone fit into the Cahill structure. Hamilton was a Tomas, which explained his brute strength, loyalty, and love of breaking things. Jonah, the multitalented artist, was a Janus, while Ian, a Lucian, excelled at anything having to do with manipulating people or money or both. But the Ekats were inventors and scientists. Sinead Starling was one and so was Cara. It made sense to send her.

"Okay, the four of you go," Dan told them. "But no canoodling. Take the private plane and see what Ted and Ned know about Sinead. Maybe she'll even be there and this'll be over fast?"

"I think the CIA would have found her if she was still at her house with her brothers," Cara suggested. "They're not terrible at their jobs."

"They let a teenager steal samples of an experimental pox virus," said Dan. "And asked other teenagers to get it back."

"Okay," Cara conceded. "But they're not *that* terrible at their jobs. They're probably watching the house already."

"Good," said Dan. "Then they'll see how the real secret agents work. As for us"—he turned to his sister—"we can get Nellie to watch the house and feed Saladin."

The cat purred at the sound of his own name, then went back to napping in the sunbeam on Ian's pants.

"What are we going to do?" Amy asked Dan. She rested a finger on her place on the page.

"We're going to Havana," said Dan. "We're going to find this Dr. Don Miller and learn what this virus he designed is meant to do and why Sinead would want to steal it."

"I've always wanted to go to Cuba," Amy said. "It has a fascinating history."

"History," Dan groaned. He was far more interested in baseball, for which the island of Cuba was famous. He hoped there'd be time to catch a game, or at least pick up some Cuban baseball cards. Saving the world was their job, but Dan wasn't about to give up on his hobbies.

CHAPTER 8

Somewhere over the Atlantic Ocean

Amy had always dreamed of traveling to Cuba, but it had been illegal for most of her life. It was only in the last few years that the United States reopened an embassy there. For a long time, the two nations, which sit just ninety miles from each other, remained in a state of perpetual cold war.

Cuba had been a close ally of the United States, but the former dictator, Fulgencio Batista, abused his power and the people rose up against him. In 1959, a young revolutionary named Fidel Castro led a violent uprising that overthrew the government, seized private property, and transformed Cuba into a Communist country, where the state owned and controlled everything, from homes and businesses to farms and factories. Even the newspapers, radio, and television stations were controlled by the Castro government. They became allies of the Soviet Union and sworn enemies of the United States. The CIA tried to poison one of Fidel Castro's cigars to get rid of him, but the plot failed. Amy suspected the Lucians had been involved in that twisted idea.

The two countries may have been only ninety miles apart, but they were worlds away. As the United States prospered in the twentieth and twenty-first centuries, Cuba struggled in isolation.

Amy was surprised to find a forty-five-minute flight from sunny Miami to sunny Havana, Cuba's capital, and she'd booked two seats. Relations between the US and Cuba were improving. Was it a coincidence that the plots and coups and assassination attempts had stopped when Amy and Dan had taken over the Cahill leadership?

"It's not a free country, though," she explained to Dan. "They like tourists, but still, it's a Communist dictatorship. The president is Fidel Castro's brother, Raúl, and he hasn't forgotten how the US tried to assassinate Fidel. Our countries don't exactly trust each other."

"Seems fitting, then," said Dan. Amy wasn't sure what he meant. "That we're on Sinead's trail to a place like that, where people don't trust each other."

Amy frowned. Dan had already decided Sinead was guilty of something terrible. Amy was the one who Sinead had attacked, but Dan was the one who couldn't forgive. Her brother could be so stubborn sometimes. It was endearing when he stubbornly refused to clean his room. It was scary when he stubbornly held on to a grudge.

As Amy tried to tell him more about Cuban history for the rest of their flight, Dan was more interested in the history of Cuban baseball: how retired Cuban dictator Fidel Castro was scouted by a major league baseball team in the '50s and might never have led the Cuban revolution if he'd just been a better pitcher.

"That turned out not to be true," Amy told him. "It was just a myth."

"But baseball is popular in Cuba just like in America," Dan pointed out. "Baseball came to Cuba in 1864 when a college student named Nemesio Guillot brought it to the island from Alabama. Nemesio was one of us. From the Tomas branch of the family."

"That's great, Dan," Amy said. "But it's not so important right now. What *is* important is finding Dr. Miller. If he defected from the US, they'd probably want to keep him under guard, so he's somewhere in the capital, close to the center of power. If he's still practicing medicine, other doctors probably know him. We should start asking around at the hospitals."

"You're missing my point," Dan said. "There have been Cahills in Cuba since at least 1864. There are definitely some there now. We don't need to go hanging around hospitals asking questions. We run the family. We can just find our contacts and get them to tell us what they know."

Dan pulled out his phone. Cara had uploaded the Cahill family directory into his contacts. He put his thumb to the screen, which would only unlock with his thumbprint. Then the camera scanned his eye for a double match, and only then could he access the data. He had to do the same thing if he wanted to play CandySmash, which was kind of a pain, but at least it meant no one could hack his contact list when he left the phone lying around, which Amy knew he would. Her brother would misplace his own face if it wasn't stuck to the front of his head.

This job wasn't like their others, though. This job was personal, and it was starting to feel a bit like their old adventures: someone in the Cahill network doing something devious for unknown reasons, and Amy and her brother having to get to the bottom of it before disaster struck. She didn't like the sense that they'd been through this before. She didn't like the idea that their moves might be predictable, that they might be falling right into a trap. They needed to gain the element of surprise.

"Great!" Dan smiled down at his phone. "Looks like there's a doctor named Jorge Neuman, who is the head of the department of infectious diseases at the medical school in Havana *and* the director of the Cuban Ministry of Health. And he just happens to be a . . ." Dan wrinkled his brow. Snorted. "A Lucian."

Amy cocked her head. "Not an Ekat?"

"It says right here. 'Dr. Jorge Neuman, Lucian.'" Dan tapped the screen. "I mean, he must be political, to be in charge of the health ministry. He has a lot of power in Cuba. But he hasn't been active in the family since . . . wow, October 1962."

"The Cuban Missile Crisis," Amy replied. "The Soviet Union put nuclear missiles in Cuba so they could strike the US if we ever tried to invade."

"Wait? There were nuclear missiles aimed at us ninety miles from Florida?" Dan asked.

"Yep," said Amy. "They were armed and ready to fire, and the US Air Force was prepared to return fire. It was almost full thermonuclear war. Kids as far away as Boston were being taught to hide under the desks when the nuclear blast came."

"That's nuts," said Dan. "A school desk can't protect you from a nuclear explosion."

"No one knew what to do," said Amy. "Secret conversations were happening to try to stop the tension, but some generals in the US and in Cuba actually *wanted* the war. Luckily, both sides backed down and the missiles were removed, but the US and Cuba cut off all relations from then on. They never trusted each other again. It was the closest humanity came to wiping itself out."

"I guess Dr. Neuman chose to be on the Cuban side," Dan said. "I'm sure Grace was *thrilled* about that."

Grace Cahill, Dan and Amy's grandmother, had been in charge of the family until she passed away a few years ago, and she had strict expectations for all the important members of the vast family network. Choosing sides against her was a very dangerous thing to do.

Then again, choosing sides against Amy and Dan had proven to be just as dangerous.

"I bet Dr. Neuman still knows what's going on," said Dan. "I bet he can tell us exactly where this Dr. Miller is hiding. He's probably running the whole dirty business from retirement. Once a Lucian, always a Lucian."

"You really have a hard time trusting people," said Amy.

"Well, yeah," said Dan. "Doesn't it seem like every time we meet someone new, they end up being the very people who are trying to destroy us?"

"Yeah," Amy agreed. "But maybe this time will be different."

"Why's that?" Dan wondered.

Amy thought about it for a moment. "Because this time, we're not the ones being hunted," she said. "This time, we're the hunters."

CHAPTER 9

Berkeley, England

Berkeley, England, was indeed as quaint as Ian had told Ham it would be. There were squat little brick houses with sloped tile roofs on neat narrow streets with little hedgerows beside them. The church tower of St. Mary's poked above the rooftops, and the nine-hundred-year-old Berkeley Castle looked over the town in serene silence. Birds chirped in the trees and a man in a tweed jacket wobbled past them on an old bicycle. Everything was neat and everything was tidy and everything was boring.

It made Ham want to put his fist through something. "This place is trying too hard to be British," he said.

"I assure you," Ian replied, "it is not trying to be anything at all. It probably looks now just like it did a hundred years ago."

As they strolled along the lane out of town that led to the Starlings' last-known address, Ham spotted a neatly tended field where the local rugby club was practicing. The bright green grass gleamed with morning dew.

At the sound of a whistle, the rugby players pulled and tore at one another in the scrum, grunting and shouting. Unlike in American football, rugby was played without pads, and the sounds one heard were not the plastic-on-plastic impact of helmets but the slap of flesh and the crunch of bone.

"Maybe this place isn't so bad after all," Ham mused. He wondered about joining a rugby league back home, maybe playing in college. He hadn't broken a bone—his own or anyone else's—in months, and he was getting antsy.

"Come along." Ian nudged him past the field. "You can stare at the rugby team on your own time."

Even when he wasn't in charge, Ian had a way of bossing Ham around that he did not appreciate. Brit-fuff-fuff could really get on his nerves.

They arrived at the house, which was a small stone cottage with a tiled roof, like all the others in town. It sat on its own, set back from the road along a wide path with high hedges around for privacy. Ham was trying to figure out what bothered him about the path, when Ian shook his head.

"This is not right," said Ian. "This path is wide enough for a lorry, but these little cottages don't have driveways. Or they don't usually. Someone cleared this recently so that large vehicles could drive up to the door directly."

"You live in America," Ham told him. "We call them trucks, not lorries."

"We are presently in England, Hamilton," Ian said back to him. "And I will call them by their proper name. *We* invented the English language after all."

"Yeah, but we made it better," Ham told him.

"You brutalized it, you mean."

Ham narrowed his eyes at Ian. "Hey, some things from England need to get brutalized every now and then."

"Of course your only answer to a superior intellect is to hit something," Ian scoffed.

Cara stepped between them.

"You both speak English just fine," she said. "Ham, it's fine you like to hit things. Ian, we're all very impressed by the size of your intellect, but since we're all on the same side, why don't we calm down a bit?"

"I'm calm," said Ham, staring at Ian.

"I am a sea of serenity," Ian replied with a grin that made Ham want to knock his teeth in.

"No one's home," Jonah told them. He'd knocked on the door and peered inside the windows while they'd been arguing. "Door's locked."

"I can pick the lock," Cara volunteered, removing a small lock-picking set from her canvas backpack.

"I got this," Ham told her, stepping to the door before she reached it. He looked at the door frame for a second, wound up, and delivered a satisfying kick right next to the doorknob.

The door burst open with a crack and splinter of wood.

"Why . . . why would you do that?!" Ian exclaimed.

Ham shrugged. "Sometimes you just gotta hit something, you know?"

He stepped inside first to make sure the place was clear. Standard security procedure. Motion sensors activated the lights, and somewhere, a generator switched on. The place wasn't connected to the local power grid. It made its own power.

When he was satisfied the cottage was empty, he called out, "Clear!" and the others came in.

"Sick pad," Jonah said, speaking loudly over the hum of the generator.

"This is unexpected," Ian said.

"What the—" Cara said.

Ham hadn't really been looking at the strange- ness of the cottage's insides when he was scanning the room. Now, seeing it through the others' eyes, he took in what was so odd about it.

From the outside it was a nineteenth-century workman's cottage. From the inside, it looked like a state-of-the-art Biosafety Level Four containment laboratory. Two-thirds of the cottage was on the other side of a wall of thick glass. There were lab tables and microscopes, pipettes and centrifuges, freezers and ovens, large tanks of various gases, and racks of vials and beakers. There were also sealed glass containers that held what looked like caterpillars, hundreds of them, all crawling and climbing the sides of their tanks, hanging upside down from the lids and struggling over one another as if they were competing to see which one could occupy the highest point in their caterpillar prison.

On the kids' side of the glass, there was a row of lockers directly in front of them, with a sealed door that led to a decontamination shower. On the other side of the shower was the entry door into the laboratory. You couldn't get in or out without first being sprayed with chemicals.

"What's missing?" Jonah asked.

Ham looked around again. It seemed like a pretty thorough setup for an experimental lab.

"A bed," said Ian. "A kitchen. Chairs. The Starlings do not live here."

"No one lives here," Cara agreed.

"Stay on your guard," Ian warned.

Ham didn't need to be told. He always stayed on his guard.

Ian was right that the finer points of the intellect didn't concern Ham so much. He wasn't dumb, he just didn't care about talking. He cared about doing whatever he needed to do to keep his people safe, even Ian. Ian might be an arrogant self-centered fop, but he was a Cahill arrogant self-centered fop, and Ham was nothing if not loyal.

They moved farther inside, looking for any hints as to what kind of work was being done in this lab. There was a computer and he booted it up.

"Encrypted," he said, and got to work trying to access it. There were three things he was good at in this world—sports, computer hacking, and knitting. He wasn't on a team right now and he'd been kicked out of the high school knitting club years ago. He was relieved he got to do at least one thing he enjoyed today.

File   Edit   View   Help

STARLING ONLY

NO ONE SNEAKS PAST
OUR DEFENSES

"Give me a shot." Cara nudged him out of the way. She was a better hacker than he was. He relented and stepped aside, cracking his knuckles.

Ham poked around the room, keeping his distance from the door to the lab itself. There was a reason that Biosafety Level Four labs had decontamination showers and sealed double doors. There was a reason people wore pressurized protective suits when they worked inside these labs. Some of the diseases that got handled in labs like this—things like anthrax, Ebola, and smallpox—could infect you with just a few tiny molecules. If you touched a doorknob with even a tiny bit of Ebola virus on it, it could get into your skin, infect your blood, and kill you in three days. One breath of an anthrax particle, and you'd start to feel a little sick by bedtime. You might never wake up.

Ham hated the idea of invisible killers like that. You couldn't beat up a virus molecule. You couldn't just fight your way through a smallpox infection with hard work and grit. If one of these diseases got you, you were at the mercy of medicine and luck.

You'd have to be crazy to set foot in a Biosafety Level Four lab.

"Should we enter the laboratory?" Ian wondered. "It seems the answers we're after will be found in there."

Brit-fuff-fuff didn't lack bravery, that was clear.

There were pictures on the walls on the other side of the glass, images of virus particles and close-ups of blood cells. Someone had been working on something in there. Cara was having no luck with the computer, but none of them made a move toward the lab.

There was a whiteboard on the other side of the glass, and it had handwriting on it that Ham recognized. Sinead's.

25.0000° N, 71.0000° W, it read.

"What is that?" he asked.

"Geographic coordinates," said Ian.

"For the Bermuda Triangle," said Cara. "A patch of ocean in the Atlantic rumored to be where ships and airplanes mysteriously disappear." She shook her head. "But it's just a myth. In truth, ships and planes cross it all the time without problems. It's four hundred miles from the coast of Cuba in one of the busiest shipping lanes in the world."

"Then why would Sinead have written down those coordinates?" Ham asked.

"It's where the most secure Ekat stronghold was," Cara said. "No outsider has ever infiltrated it. Heck, I've never even been."

"Sinead, like you, is an Ekat," said Ian.

"The Ekat base is abandoned," Cara said. "It was built by Marie Curie to house her secret lab, but after the clue hunt and the destruction of the former Cahill leadership, the Ekats left it behind."

"It'd be a perfect place to hide," Jonah said. "With all those automatic defenses and secret labs, you could launch a virus as a weapon and hide out there for as long as you needed."

"We don't know Sinead is making a weapon," said Ham.

"We will know once I get this computer cracked," said Cara. "I just need to—"

She was cut off by the slam of car doors. They hadn't heard a vehicle approach because of the sound of the house's generator, and they had no time to hide themselves as four figures stepped inside, all of them wearing blue biohazard suits with breathing tanks attached.

The light reflecting off the masks hid their faces. For a moment, Ham thought this might be Sinead and the Starling brothers, but they were the wrong size and there were four of them.

"Hey, guys, 'sup?" Jonah asked, faking casualness in that way he had of never showing surprise. Ham stepped toward them, putting his body in front of everyone else's. "What's with the space suits?"

Ian and Cara had frozen in place. They'd seen what Jonah hadn't yet, but what Ham saw instantly.

All four of the figures in the biohazard suits were armed.

CHAPTER 10

Jonah's eyes scanned the four figures. The one in front held a black pistol in his right hand, while the two behind him had blowtorches and the fourth held a sledgehammer. Their suits were blue and hissed as they breathed. They looked like space explorers arriving on Mars.

Which made Jonah, Ian, Cara, and Ham the Martians. In sci-fi movies, things never went well for the Martians. At least they hadn't in the sci-fi movie he'd just finished filming, *RoboGangsta: Martian Mayhem.*

Jonah was still thinking about his brilliant sci-fi movie when Ham sprang into action.

His friend crossed the distance to the front door in three large strides, and on the fourth, brought a crushing two-handed hammer blow down on the first astronaut-looking goon.

"Ahh!" the man screamed, doubling over and dropping the gun, which went off as he released it.

Jonah dove to knock Ian and Cara out of the way. The single stray bullet shot into the glass wall behind them, exactly where Ian's head had been.

Jonah held his breath, but the glass hadn't broken. The lab was still sealed, whatever virus inside still contained.

He let the breath out.

Ham, meanwhile, had slammed an elbow down into the back of the gunman's head, knocking him out, while the two with the blowtorches rushed for him.

He ducked below a stream of flame and delivered a high kick into one guy's chest, knocking him backward into the man with the sledgehammer, then he head-butted the other, cracking the face plate of his suit.

"Ahhh!" the man screamed, and gripped his face as a *whoosh* of air left his suit, deflating it.

The gunman on the floor stirred and began to stand, reaching for his weapon. Cara dove for it, knocking it from the man's grasp, then delivered a scissors kick to his already battered head. The suit tore at the seam of the neck and there was a loud *whoosh* of escaping air.

Sledgehammer guy had recovered and was coming straight for Jonah. "Yo, not in the face," Jonah said, raising his arms to protect his head, which had the effect he'd wanted. The guy raised the hammer to swing straight at Jonah's face, which exposed the man's stomach and chest. Jonah delivered a quick one-two punch, then grabbed the battery pack on the side of the suit and yanked it hard, tearing open the fabric.

Whoosh.

The hammer flew from the man's grip.

"Ha!" Jonah shouted, but time felt like it slowed down as he watched the sledgehammer fly past him and connect with the spiderweb of cracking glass where the bullet had embedded itself.

When the hammer hit, the window rippled, the cracks bent and spread, and then, with a crash, the window into the lab smashed open in a rain of glass.

"Get out of here!" one of the blowtorch astronauts yelled. "The lab is breached. Our suits are compromised!"

Ian dove onto the gunman and held him down on the floor. "Who are you?" he demanded. "Where's Sinead?"

The gunman reached around and released his air hose, which sprayed high-pressure air right into Ian's face, knocking him onto his back. The man was on his feet in a flash and all four astronaut-soldiers ran for the front door.

One of the blowtorch guys let loose another spout of flame, forcing Jonah, Ian, Ham, and Cara to dive for cover on the other side of the smashed window, inside the containment lab.

The stream of fire shot across the room and the guy aimed first at the computer, torching it beyond use before he turned and fired over their heads, burning up the whiteboard. The men backed out the doorway.

As soon as they had stepped outside, Ham was on his feet again, leaping over the fires burning throughout the room. He'd never catch them. Their car was peeling out before Ham even got to the threshold. He came back panting from the sudden sprint.

"They got away," he said sadly. "A black Mercedes van, no license plate."

Ian had found a heavy-duty fire extinguisher and put out the flames.

"Did you see how quickly they ran out of here when the glass broke?" Jonah asked, his heart still pounding. "They were *not* messing around."

At that very instant, all four of them came to the same terrible realization. They looked up. They were standing on the wrong side of the shattered glass. They were standing in the wide-open laboratory.

Jonah had been resting his hand on the countertop. He pulled it away like it was burning hot. Ian dropped the fire extinguisher. Ham stopped panting.

"None of us are wearing suits," Ian said.

They all ran outside, but Jonah feared none of them could run fast enough. They'd knelt on the floor; they'd touched the counters, breathed the air, cut their fingers on the broken glass.

"Yo, we need to find out what this virus does," Jonah said. "And fast."

Ham looked at him, pale as a sheet. "I have a bad feeling we're going to find out the hard way."

Whatever that lab contained, every one of them had been exposed.

CHAPTER 11

Havana, Cuba

Dr. Neuman lived on the sixth story of a six-story building without an elevator. It was sweltering in the stairwell, and both Dan and Amy were sweating when they finally reached his apartment, which made it more annoying to find out that he wasn't home.

"No está aquí," the woman who answered the door told them, then with one glance sized them up as Americans. "My father is not home," she said in perfect English.

She didn't let them in, but they could see over her shoulder that the living room was lined with bookshelves. Instead of a couch, there was a bed and a baby's crib. Amy had said that Cubans couldn't own property—it all belonged to the government—so if someone had a big apartment, their whole extended family might end up living in it. It looked like Dr. Neuman had a full house.

"Oh, well, do you know where he is?" Dan asked.

"My father knows you?" his daughter wondered, suspicious.

Dan glanced at his sister. He decided to take a gamble. "Yeah," he said. "We're family friends. I'm Dan Cahill and this is my sister, Amy."

The woman's eyes widened. "Cahill?" she said.

"Cahill," Dan repeated.

Oh, how he liked using that name to people who'd heard of them! The Cahill name meant nothing to most people, but to some, it was better than a picklock or a battering ram. It opened doors. After all the years he and his sister had spent running from people, it felt good to put a little terror into someone else's heart. He really liked feeling as if he was, for once, in control.

Does that make me evil? he wondered.

No, he told himself. *Just confident. I'm Dan Cahill and I do what needs to be done.*

The woman wrinkled her forehead, frowned, then took a deep breath. "He said you would come one day," she told them. "He used to tell me stories about the power of the Cahill family. When we were starving in the nineties after the Soviet Union collapsed, he would describe the feasts at the family mansion so that we could imagine the food on our table was so delicious, rather than boiled grapefruit peels. My mother scolded him for his nostalgia. He had chosen the revolution, after all, and cut ties with the Cahills. Why should he look backward? But still, I knew he always did."

"We really need to talk to him," Dan said. "Urgent family business."

"Urgent?" she said. "How urgent could it be if they have sent children?"

"I'm *Dan* Cahill," Dan repeated. "This is *Amy*?" Their first names meant nothing to this woman. So much for feeling powerful. "We're, like, in charge of the whole family!"

"You two?" The woman's eyebrows shot up. "Teenagers? In charge? Of the most powerful family in history?"

Dan nodded.

"What happened to the adults?"

"We've proven ourselves incorruptible," Amy said, joining the conversation. Dan had been beginning to worry she'd gone mute. "Unlike the adults."

The woman nodded. This seemed convincing enough to her. Even though everyone in Cuba was supposed to be equal because of Communism, some government ministers lived in big homes all to themselves, while other ministers—maybe ones who didn't take bribes—lived in sixth-floor apartments with their children and grandchildren.

"So you are here because of the outbreak?" Dr. Neuman's daughter asked.

Amy took a quick breath in and Dan's pulse jumped. *The outbreak? Here?* His heart raced. He'd planned to track down the scientist who'd manipulated the goat pox virus and use him to find Sinead. He hadn't planned on stepping into the middle of some actual outbreak of a disease. The whole point of this job was to *stop* an outbreak from happening.

"They called my father into the hospital," the woman said. "Hundreds of young people with strange symptoms. None of the staff doctors knew what to do." She disappeared from the doorway for a moment and came back with a bag of bright red pills.

"Please bring this to him," she said. "He will make time for you if you have these."

"Are they medicine?" Dan asked, and the woman cracked a smile for the first time.

"No, of course not! They are Red Hots! Cinnamon candies. My father has a sweet tooth, especially when he is working."

The Hermanos Ameijeiras Hospital was a massive building in the Centro neighborhood of Havana, just a short walk from the doctor's apartment. It was a tall square building of old pink concrete with straight rows of dirty glass windows. They could see it from the street when they stepped outside, as it towered over the rest of the neighborhood. It wasn't pretty, but it was huge.

They rushed through the business district, past classic cars from the 1950s and 1960s that were used as taxis, past pastel-colored buildings from the same era. It was as if the city of Havana had been stuck in time from the decade after the revolution that put Fidel Castro in power and caused the United States to cut off all relations with the island. Life had gone on for all those years, of course, but it seemed as if new building had stopped.

Palm trees swayed in the evening breeze and music blared from boom boxes. Old men sat playing dominoes at card tables on the sidewalk. Kids played baseball in the middle of the street. Dan noticed one strange thing, though: Over some doorways, there was a stenciled image of a figure with an eyeball for a head, wielding a large sword. The letters *CDR* were stenciled next to it.

"That's the Committee for the Defense of the Revolution," Amy explained as they went past. "Every block in Havana has one, and they maintain a file on every resident of their block. They report anything suspicious, any activity that might be counterrevolutionary, or anything that might make someone they don't like look bad."

"So every block has government spies on it?" Dan wondered.

Amy nodded, while simultaneously shushing him. "This isn't a free country," she whispered. "Talking too much can get you thrown in jail."

"Oh," said Dan, smirking. "So this is the perfect country for you. Everybody keeps to themselves."

Amy grunted a response, which was enough for Dan. She'd long ago overcome her stutter and her shyness, but he joked to break the tension, and with sword-wielding eyeball graffiti watching from every darkened doorway and a mysterious disease breaking out, he was pretty tense. Not giving-a-book-report-on-a-book-he-hadn't-read-in-front-of-the-whole-class tense, but still . . . pretty tense.

They were two blocks away from the hospital when they reached the first police blockade.

An officer said something to him and waved them away.

"*No hablo español*," Dan told him, which was how you said you didn't speak Spanish in Spanish. He always thought it was weird to tell someone you didn't speak their language in their own language, because you were speaking it as you told them you couldn't. It was a logic problem that would have to bother him another time, though. "We need to see Dr. Neuman," he said in English. "Dr. Jorge Neuman?"

The police officer looked Dan and Amy over, his brow furrowed deeply.

Then Dan held up the bag of Red Hots. "Dr. Jorge Neuman needs these right away!"

"Eh!" one of the other police officers shouted when he saw the Red Hots. "Dr. Neuman! ¡Sí! ¡Sí!" He waved them through the blockade quickly. "¡Apúrate! ¡Vamos!"

Dan and Amy ran past him and sprinted all the way to the hospital entrance, with police radioing ahead to clear their path. When they reached the big entrance doors labeled *Emergencia*, a nurse wearing a surgical mask was waiting for them.

"You have Dr. Neuman's candies?" she demanded curtly, her hand already extended to take them.

Dan pulled them back from her. "We need to see him," he told the woman.

"No," she said through her mask. "No admittance."

"Sorry," Dan said. "We *have* to talk to him. If he wants his candies, he has to at least come get them himself. Tell him Dan and Amy *Cahill* are here. Got that? Cahill."

Dan crossed his arms, protecting the bag of candies against his chest. He waited.

The nurse's mask billowed out and then sucked in with her angry breathing. Finally, she rolled her eyes and held up a finger, telling them to stay put. She rushed inside the hospital again.

"I've never held cinnamon candy hostage before," Dan said.

"Dr. Neuman must *really* like Red Hots," Amy noted.

"Like Saladin and his red snapper," Dan added.

"Maybe don't compare a renowned doctor to a pet cat," Amy suggested.

Dan shrugged. "I don't think Saladin thinks he's a pet."

Just then, the nurse came out and handed them each blue surgical coveralls, complete with hoods; surgical masks; two pairs of rubber gloves apiece; rubber overshoes; and plastic goggles.

"Put on," she said.

Amy gave Dan a nervous look, which Dan returned. They were supposed to go into the hospital? They didn't have training. They weren't doctors or nurses. If there was an outbreak going on, wouldn't it have been better for the doctor to come out and meet them?

"Put on," the nurse repeated. "He is waiting."

They began covering themselves in the sterile protective clothing. The nurse checked them over, taping their sleeves around their gloves and their pant legs around their rubber overshoes. She made sure they had no skin exposed anywhere on their bodies.

"Is it really that contagious?" Dan asked. The nurse just nodded.

He double-checked the seals at his cuffs and ankles, and made sure his gloves weren't ripped.

Once the nurse was satisfied, she told them to follow her. "You come inside," she said. "And don't touch *anything*. Everything inside is contaminated. A . . . you call it . . . a hot zone."

Dan felt suddenly cold.

A hot zone. Infection. Why had he volunteered them for this job? Sinead was never good news. He should've known better.

He pictured the horrors that waited for them on the other side of the hospital doors. He imagined zombie outbreaks and running for their lives from invisible virus particles. He imagined a stench of sickness so powerful it would never wash off.

What he did not expect to see as they stepped through the doors into the brightly lit halls of the emergency room was a dance party.

CHAPTER 12

There was no music, but everywhere Amy looked, there were young people dancing.

The lobby was a grand space of marble and tile, and potted plants formed borders around waiting areas holding red modernist furniture. It was far nicer than she had imagined a Cuban hospital would be, and she remembered that the Hermanos Ameijeiras Hospital was the premier hospital for the entire country.

Except it looked more like a bizzaro night club. Teenagers danced on the potted plants and bopped on top of the furniture. Their bodies bounced, their legs did the twist, and their feet stomped, while their hips and shoulders shimmied.

Nurses and doctors covered head to toe in protective suits tried to make the teenagers sit down, but every time they drew close the teenagers flailed wildly, tearing at the medical staff as if they were being attacked.

"Okay," said Dan, his voice muffled through the surgical mask. "This is weird."

Amy agreed.

"Come quickly," the nurse urged them, and they moved through the lobby to the elevators. When they reached the fluorescent-lit halls of the infectious disease ward, there were still more dancers.

Amy peered behind curtains and saw kids in hospital gowns standing on their beds pumping their fists in the air and jumping up and down like they were at one of Jonah's concerts. Frantic adults pleaded with them to come down, but the waving arms and kicking legs pushed them back. The adults were being careful not to tear their sterile outfits. They were trying not to touch the dancers.

At the end of the hall sat a group of teens in a drum circle, except they had no drums. They swatted the air in front of them, jumping and swaying to their own beat, and as they drummed, their heads jerked this way and that, sweat flying off them in great salty arcs.

"Look at their faces," Dan said, and Amy saw that every single dancer, dripping with sweat and moving to imaginary music, had the same expression on his or her face. Their jaws were wide open, their eyebrows raised, and their eyes wide. It looked like each of them was screaming without making any sound. They all looked terrified.

Dan and Amy stopped outside one room, where two orderlies had strapped down a teenager to stop her from dancing. She was thrashing wildly, and the heart monitor they'd attached sounded an alarm. They tried to inject her with something, but they couldn't get her still enough for the needle.

And then the girl's heart stopped.

The nurses shouted, and a doctor came running. There was a frantic conversation and the orderlies undid the straps.

Almost instantly, the girl's arms and legs twitched free and her heart started again. She began to dance on the bed, then popped up to her knees, and then stood, doing a samba.

"If they stop dancing, they die," Dan observed.

Amy looked back down the hall at the silent drum circle, at the boys and girls all around grooving to their own beat. She shuddered.

In the room, the girl on the bed whipped her hair back and forth and streams of sweat splashed across the goggles and surgical mask of one of the orderlies. He jumped back as if he'd been shot. The doctor and the other orderly stepped away from him.

"*That* is how it spreads," a man behind Amy said. "Through the sweat. The sweat is loaded with virus particles. As they dance, they sweat, and the sweat flies off them and the virus becomes airborne."

Amy turned to see a small figure, covered, like she was, from head to toe in a blue protective suit. Beneath his goggles, however, she could see his bright white eyebrows, so bushy that the hairs were smashed against the plastic, and it gave the impression of two caterpillars trying to escape a classroom terrarium.

"Dr. Neuman?" Dan asked.

"Do you have my Red Hots?" he replied.

Dan handed the man the plastic bag, which the old doctor looked at with a smile in his eyes. Amy assumed it was a smile. Not being able to see anything but his eyes, she actually couldn't tell.

"Come to my office," he said. "We can have a snack while you tell me what brought you to our island in the midst of a most unusual crisis."

"I'm not very hungry," Amy told the doctor, her appetite having vanished the moment she stepped into the hospital.

"I could eat," Dan said, which was about as true a statement as she'd ever heard. Nothing could stop her little brother from snacking.

They passed through a decontamination shower and what the doctor called a "gray room," which was a room between the clean zones where every possible particle of virus had been killed before entering, and the "hot zones," like the emergency area, where the virus was everywhere and the possibility of infection was high.

Cuba had some of the best medical care in Latin America, in spite of being an isolated island, and Dr. Neuman was very proud of the decontamination system he had built.

"We meet all the Biosafety Level Four protocols," he explained as one of his aides tossed their jumpsuits directly into an incinerator chute.

Once more in their civilian clothes, they sat in the doctor's office, staring across his wide steel desk and out the window behind him, which overlooked Havana all the way to the seaside promenade and across the Gulf of Mexico toward Florida.

"So you are Grace Cahill's grandchildren," Dr. Neuman said. "I had heard that teenagers were now leading the family, but to see it with my own eyes . . ." He laughed and slapped his palms on his desk. "Let me guess . . . the adults let ambition and greed so consume them that only through children could the family remain united?"

Amy and Dan looked at each other, surprised by how well this old doctor understood what had happened. Amy felt a little proud of having united the family in such a way that even this doctor had heard of them. She sat a little straighter in her chair.

"Long ago, I chose my country over my loyalty to your grandmother and her vision of greatness," Dr. Neuman said. "I saw the injustice my people faced in Cuba and I joined the revolution."

He nodded toward a framed photo of Fidel Castro, the dictator who had taken over Cuba in 1959 and had ruled it with a fist for the last sixty years, lately through his younger brother Raúl.

"Unlike you decadent capitalists, our country takes care of its own," the doctor said, and all kindness left his eyes. He was obviously committed to the idea that the United States was an enemy nation, and Amy knew she would have to tread carefully if they wanted his help finding Dr. Miller.

"We are a nation of ideals." Dr. Neuman pounded his desk. "We are willing to suffer for the greater good, while you *Americans*"—he said the word *Americans* as if it were an insult—"want only the next video game or fancy car. Materialistic! Selfish! I have dedicated my life to serving the people of Cuba and the global Communist movement . . . and yet now . . . you come to me just as this strange new disease emerges in my country. I cannot help but think you have brought this here. I cannot help but think this is an attack on my country."

"We're here to stop this disease," Dan objected. "We don't care about your politics or your revolution. We just want to prevent an outbreak of . . . whatever this is."

"You don't even know what this disease is, do you?" Dr. Neuman asked.

"Not really," said Amy, before Dan could answer. She didn't want her brother to say anything about the US government sending them. The doctor might not help them if he thought they worked for the CIA. She'd also found that a certain kind of man liked to think he was smarter than everyone else, and couldn't resist explaining things to a teenage girl like Amy. All she had to do was give him an excuse to show his expertise. "Could you explain this to us? We don't understand what we're seeing."

The doctor nodded sadly. "In southern Italy during the seventeenth century, there was an outbreak of something called *tarantism*," he told them. "Villagers, usually peasants, would erupt in uncontrollable fits of dancing, for hours, sometimes for days, wearing themselves out. The dancing fits spread throughout the region and their cause was never quite identified. The phenomenon gave rise to a dance called the tarantella, but otherwise, this odd outbreak was forgotten by history."

"So you think this is a return of a seventeenth-century Italian disease?" Amy asked.

The doctor shook his head. "No, I think this is an entirely new virus pretending to be something much older. It is quite ingenious." He pulled out a large plastic model of a molecule. "This is a model of a virus particle called *virion*," he explained. "A smallpox virion, in fact."

Amy sat up straighter, studying the large model.

"The outer layer is the protein coat, which protects the genetic material of the virus inside the nucleic acid at its core. When a particle attaches to a host cell, the protein coat dissolves and the genetic material inside infects the host cell, reproducing itself, until that cell is either killed or transformed. It repeats this process over and over and over again. Like all forms of life, it wants itself to thrive. It spreads and reproduces. The more successful viruses find ingenious ways of spreading from host to host, whether through the air by being inhaled or settling on the skin or being contained in bodily fluids."

"Like sweat," said Amy.

"Like sweat," the doctor agreed. "This outbreak in my emergency room downstairs is like nothing I have ever seen before," he told them. He pulled out a photo taken from a microscope. "This is from one of the patients downstairs. This is the virus they are all infected with."

Amy looked but couldn't make much sense of it. There were virus particles shaped like little bricks attached to flat, disclike particles she recognized from biology class as blood cells.

"The shape of the virus is identical to goat pox," he said. "A pox virus that is harmless to humans." Amy shifted uncomfortably in her seat. She could tell this version of it wasn't harmless at all. In her mind, she still heard the loud beep of the poor girl's stopped heart until she was allowed to dance again. "As far as my early examinations show," the doctor continued, "the genetic material inside is a type of baculovirus."

"A back-u-what virus?" Dan asked. "You're losing me."

"A baculovirus is a type of virus that only infects invertebrates—moths and caterpillars and beetles," the doctor explained. "There is a specific baculovirus in Brazil called the climbing virus. When active in a caterpillar, it changes the creature's behavior, turning it into a kind of zombie with only one thought: to climb."

"Zombies?" Dan gasped. Amy's brother loved video games and TV shows about zombies, but she could see his confidence waver at the thought of facing real-life zombies.

"Not like imaginary brain-eating zombies," Dr. Neuman said. "Infected caterpillars climb up into the treetops and wait there until they die, at which point they melt into liquid, which drips down from the treetops. The liquid is loaded with the virus and the caterpillars on the forest floor below are infected, thus continuing the cycle."

Amy felt sick to her stomach, picturing infected caterpillar goo raining from the treetops, but Dan happily munched away at the cinnamon candies. His momentary fear of zombies had vanished when he'd heard his brains were safe. Amy's fear amped up. She knew that nature could conjure more horrors than anything a Hollywood studio could dream up.

"My best guess right now," Dr. Neuman said, "is that the virus we see in these dancers is a baculovirus modified to infect humans and, rather than causing climbing behavior as it does in the caterpillars, it causes its victims to dance. By dancing, they spread the disease."

"Dancing doesn't seem so bad," Dan said. "I mean, like, *I* wouldn't want to be stuck dancing, but it's not the end of the world to have a bunch of sweaty teenagers dancing. Unless you're a middle-school principal."

The doctor rubbed his eyes. "Unfortunately, since they began arriving a few hours ago, none of our patients have stopped dancing. Not to rest, not to drink water, not to eat."

"Oh . . ." said Amy, realizing what he meant.

"They are going to become dehydrated and exhausted," the doctor said. "I am not certain how long a person can dance, but our best guess is it will be only another day or two, depending on their fitness before they became infected. When their bodies can no longer keep dancing, they will collapse. And then . . ."

"Their hearts will stop," said Amy.

"And if we force them to stop dancing . . ." the doctor said.

"Their hearts stop sooner," Amy finished his sentence.

"Whoa," said Dan. "You mean they're going to dance themselves to *death*?"

The doctor held his palms up in the air. "The virus is like nothing I've seen before. The protein shell from the pox virus protects it from any inoculation we have, and the genetic structures in the nucleic acid are completely unfamiliar to us. It will take months of research simply to understand it, let alone to develop a cure. I fear the fatality rate will be catastrophic long before then. Already, three of my staff have become infected. One of them is quite an admirable salsa dancer, and it would be a pleasure to watch her, if I was not afraid she was going to die of it."

"Sick," Dan muttered.

Amy pictured Sinead, her bright red hair, her preppy outfits, and she wondered how such a girl could be involved with something so terrible. Why had she stolen this virus from its lab? And who had unleashed it on the unfortunate youth of Havana?

Her anger bubbled up inside her. If it was Sinead, then perhaps Dan was right. She was unforgivable.

"Now I have told you what I know," said Dr. Neuman. "Why don't you explain to me, at last, how it is *you* are involved and how you two intend to help?"

"We're looking for another doctor," Amy said, showing him the picture of Dr. Miller she had on her phone. "We believe he . . . well . . . we think he might have created this virus."

"Dr. Miller," Dr. Neuman said, nodding. "Yes, I know him, but he is forbidden from practicing medicine in Cuba. I made that a condition for him to be allowed into the country."

"You know what he used to do?" Dan asked.

The doctor nodded. "I know he did research for your government on biological weapons."

"And you didn't think he could be involved in this?" Dan was getting angry and impatient, and Amy had to put her hand on his knee to calm him down.

"*This*," the doctor replied sternly, "has only been happening for a few hours. I have not had time to think of anything but how to save my patients."

"We understand," said Amy. "Please, let us go to Dr. Miller and find out what he knows. If he created this disease, maybe he knows how to cure it."

Dr. Neuman scribbled an address on the back of his business card and handed it to Amy.

"That's in Old Havana," the doctor explained. "You will find him there. Bring him to me."

"Is this his house?" Amy asked.

Dr. Neuman shook his head. "No, it's not. . . . But if you like jazz, you should feel right at home."

CHAPTER 13

Attleboro, Massachusetts

Nellie Gomez was excited to have the night off. Her restaurant was closed for cleaning—thanks to Dan's plan—and she had her first evening free in ages. Her boyfriend, Sammy, was away at a conference, the kiddos were down in Havana, and she had the house to herself. She decided to blast some celebratory metal. She never really got to rock out when the house was full.

Things were going pretty well for her. A very important food blogger had called her cooking "the most exciting new cuisine on the restaurant scene in years," and the *Boston Globe* had just that morning declared her desserts "worth braving gunfire for."

In spite of the danger and drama in her dining room, the restaurant was fully booked for reservations for the next six months with customers itching to try her experimental dishes. She'd stuffed a duck breast with Pop Rocks and slow roasted it overnight. She'd designed a dessert tower with a molten chili-chocolate orb balanced on top. One ate it by piercing the orb and letting the chocolate flow down over the raspberry-stuffed *choux* pastry below. She even got Sammy to use his chemistry expertise to help her design whole new ways of serving food.

There had been a few setbacks.

Sushi foam wasn't as popular as she'd hoped, and she'd nearly burned off all her brightly colored hair when she'd tried to turn a beef Wellington into jelly form.

But even as the excitement over her restaurant delighted her, once she was alone with Saladin in the Attleboro mansion, her thoughts turned to worry for her kiddos down in Havana. She knew they could take care of themselves, but she wished they had brought her along. Neither Dan nor Amy even spoke Spanish.

"What do you think, Saladin?" she asked the cat, who allowed himself to be stroked by Nellie and purred contently on her lap. "You think they'll be okay?"

The cat stopped purring, then looked up at her. He cocked his head and then charged from her lap, racing down the hall.

Nellie knew the cat had a strong sense of danger, so she got up to follow him. Just as she did, the house's perimeter alarm sounded.

Someone was trying to break in.

Nellie slid open the secret door behind the bookcase and entered the high-tech control room, where she could access not only the mansion's vast security network but the entire global Cahill network—strongholds around the world, satellite feeds and weather stations, databases from intelligence agencies and law enforcement in two dozen countries. They had built quite a system after they'd rebuilt the mansion from burned cinders.

"The A-Team never had a room like this," Dan liked to joke, except Nellie knew he had never actually seen *The A-Team*.

She switched on the monitors and checked the front drive. The gate was wide open.

Whoever had come in knew the code.

But she wondered how, then, they had tripped the house alarm.

She scanned through the camera feeds, looking for the intruder. At her feet, Saladin meowed and paced below the console.

Panning a camera around the garage, she saw a car that hadn't been there before: Ian's black Tesla, its doors wide open.

Something was wrong.

Nellie spotted movement on the corner of the screen and moved the camera around the large garage to focus on it. Her hand froze over the controls, not certain what it was she was looking at.

Ham, Jonah, Ian, and Cara were all there in the garage.

Nellie hit the intercom button. "Hey, guys, it's Nellie," she said. "What are you doing in there? When did you get back?"

"Don't come down here!" Cara shouted up toward the camera. "Something happened in England! We were exposed to some sort of virus. We took Jonah's private jet back and I drove us here as fast as I could. I didn't know where else to go."

"Okay," Nellie said, worried by the alarm in Cara's voice but also quite confused. "Tell me what happened and I'll do whatever I can to help. But I have one question." She paused and tried to think of a way to ask what she'd been wondering since she'd turned the camera toward them. "Why are Ham, Jonah, and Ian dancing?"

CHAPTER 14

Havana, Cuba

The streets of Old Havana were narrow and winding, and the sunset bathed everything in pink light and purple shadow. Colorful washing hung on lines between colonial-era buildings, and tourists from China and Russia and Venezuela and Spain wandered this way and that, taking pictures of the classic cars, candy-colored shutters, and men playing dominoes.

And yet on every block, there was the image of the eye wielding a sword, the Committee for the Defense of the Revolution. Amy couldn't shake the feeling that she and her brother were being watched. If Dr. Miller didn't come with them, would Dr. Neuman collect him in some other way? If he fell into the hands of the police, they'd never get to talk to him.

Did it matter when so many lives were at stake? If he could cure the disease, wasn't that the most important thing?

Still, Sinead's involvement nagged at Amy like an itch she couldn't scratch. She needed to know: Was Sinead innocent or guilty, a good guy or a bad guy?

She hated the uncertainty. At least Dan knew what he thought of Sinead. She was still a mystery to Amy, and Amy hated leaving mysteries unsolved.

They arrived at the jazz club where they were supposed to find Dr. Miller. Even though they were young, no one looked askance at them as they stepped inside. The club was a small indoor area with a bar along one wall and a row of tables along the other, and the entire rear wall opened up to the courtyard. The courtyard had a stage and dance floor and more tables.

The tables were full and the dance floor was packed, and the band on stage was playing a wild jazz number. Three old men played saxophones and two more played trumpets. There were two guitarists and a drummer and a woman in a red dress dancing in front of the microphone, holding it like she was about to sing but had instead been carried away by the music.

It was hard to stand still listening to it. The melodies rose and fell, notes dissolving into each other and instruments passing around the rhythm as if they were playing a game of catch. Amy noticed Dan shifting his weight from foot to foot, bopping his head a little bit with the beat. It amazed Amy how much music could behave like a virus, spreading from person to person, ear to ear, and making their bodies do things that their minds didn't decide to do. She also marveled how devious it was that this strange virus they'd seen could act like music, forcing people to dance to a tune only they could hear.

The woman began to sing, a song that sounded sad and happy at the same time.

Dos gardenias para tí,
Con ellas quiero decir,
Te quiero, te adoro, mi vida.

Just as the heartache of the song swelled, a trumpet solo cut in, turning the sadness into something glorious.

"That's Dr. Miller," Dan pointed out, and Amy realized her eyes had been closed, so transported had she been by the music. She opened them to see that the trumpet player was the very man from the pictures the CIA had shown them.

"He's good," Dan added, but the thought made Amy shudder. This was a man who knew how to make people dance with music, who clearly loved it, and yet he might have created the very virus that was killing people with dancing.

At the end of the song, the crowd applauded and the musicians stopped to take a break. Dan and Amy wove their way through the crowd to the stage, where Dr. Miller had opened a soda and perched on a stool to drink it.

"Let me do the talking," Dan told Amy.

"I was always going to let you do the talking," Amy replied.

"Excuse me, sir?" Dan said, suddenly sounding a lot younger. "You play really well."

"Why, thank you," Dr. Miller answered, then

cocked his head in surprise. "You're American? Here?"

Dan nodded. "We just love your music."

The doctor looked slightly puzzled. Amy worried Dan was overacting.

"It's really hard not to dance to your playing," Dan said. "Do you like to make people dance?"

The doctor frowned, then glanced around the room. He took a long drink of his soda and stood to set the soda bottle on the floor. He squatted down so he could talk directly to Dan and Amy in a whisper. "Who are you kids?"

He'd gotten suspicious. He was looking around the room now, scanning all the faces. He knew he was probably being watched. Amy didn't want to play games with him. They didn't have time. With every passing second, the dancers in the hospital were closer to death.

"We're looking for our friend," Amy said. "Sinead Starling. We know you met with her, Dr. Miller. We need to know why."

"And we need to know how to cure your disease," Dan added, giving Amy a very puzzled look.

"Right," she added. Of course, she should've asked about that first. Her need to know about Sinead had clouded her judgment.

"My disease?" The doctor stroked his short black beard, like he was considering which disease they could possibly mean. Finally, he took a deep breath and dropped the puzzled act. "I thought this day would come," he told them. "I knew the CIA wouldn't let me get away so easily. I just didn't expect . . ." He looked Amy and Dan up and down. "Well, I didn't except *kids*."

"You shouldn't judge us by our age," said Dan. "We need to know about Sinead and we need to know about the virus she stole and we need to know if you can cure it. We don't have *any* time to lose."

"I understand," said Dr. Miller. He bent down and picked up his trumpet. He smiled at it sadly, his affection obvious. "I much prefer music to medicine," he said. Then he extended the instrument to Amy. "Would you hold this for me, please, while I get my things?"

As Amy reached out to take the trumpet, the doctor shoved it forward, knocking her into Dan and sending them both stumbling back onto the dance floor, at which point the doctor bolted in the other direction, leaping from the stage and running out the back of the club.

"Hey!" Dan yelled.

Amy untangled herself from her brother and ran after him, the trumpet still in her hands.

"Leave it!" Dan yelled.

She stopped, looked around, and then shoved the trumpet at the woman in the red dress.

"You're a beautiful singer," Dan told her. "Sorry about your trumpet player."

Then he grabbed Amy's shoulder and pulled her away. They ran together into the Havana night, pumping their legs as fast as they could.

Amy was not going to let this man escape, not without telling them what they needed to know. She hoped he was the sort of bad guy who spilled his guts freely, or she'd have to resort to tougher methods of persuasion. One way or another, though, he'd talk, of that Amy was certain.

First, they had to catch him.

CHAPTER 15

The doctor wasn't as fast as Dan, but he knew the streets of Old Havana, and that was an advantage.

But Dan had his own advantage. He'd studied city maps of Havana and he had a bird's-eye view of the entire neighborhood in his head.

The doctor took a hard right turn and they nearly lost him down an alley, but Dan knew if they ran to the next intersection, the doctor would emerge right in front of them.

And he did, tripping when he saw Dan and Amy round the corner.

"It's creepy how you do that," Amy panted.

"Compliment accepted," Dan replied.

The doctor veered left across a busy intersection, running scared, and Dan had to dive and roll across the wide hood of a cherry-red 1957 Corvette with bright white tires and a shining chrome grille.

The car honked and people shouted at him in Spanish words he didn't know but whose meaning was universal.

"Dan!" his sister shouted from behind him. "Watch out!"

"Little late," he said as his feet hit the pavement again.

He ran along the sidewalk, and Amy caught up with him. The doctor turned into a courtyard and Dan slowed.

"It's a dead end," he said. "Be careful."

They crept forward into the courtyard, but the doctor was gone.

Had Dan messed up? Was there some way out of this dead end he didn't know about, something that wasn't on the maps? The world did have a frustrating way of not being exactly like Dan thought it should be in his head.

They stood face-to-face with a concrete wall.

"Impossible!" Dan shouted. "How could he just vanish?"

Suddenly, a flock of pigeons burst into flight, and Dan's eyes shot to the roof. The doctor had taken the chase to the sky.

Amy was already moving for the rickety stairs at the back of the courtyard that wound their way up. Dan thought they'd take too long and that by the time they reached the roof, the doctor would've escaped.

He ran away from Amy, toward a rainspout along the side of the courtyard.

"What are you doing?" Amy called to him as she took the stairs two at a time.

"Catching up!" Dan answered, as if that explained anything.

But he knew if he told her what he was actually about to do, she would run down to stop him.

It's just parkour, he thought. *The French came up with it. How hard could it be?*

Parkour was a way of moving over complicated terrain in the fastest way possible. It meant going over, under, and through things that other people would normally go around. The only tools it required were your body and your mind, seeing paths that might be invisible to others.

It also meant a lot of jumping.

Dan ran straight for the wall of the building and jumped, pushing out his right foot to kick up the wall just as he hit it, so that he was almost running at a vertical angle. The kick gave him a few extra feet of height, which he used to grab on to the rainspout. It was slick under his fingertips and he slid down with a squeak.

His hands were too damp. He rubbed them on the dusty ground, then tried again, catching the spout and clinging to it for dear life. He gripped it on either side with the soles of his shoes, basically hugging it, except he kept the rest of his body back as a counterweight, like he was hugging someone he'd rather not get too close to. He took a deep breath and scurried up the spout hand over hand and foot over foot like a monkey climbing a coconut tree.

It looked a lot easier when he'd watched parkour videos on the Internet.

His feet tingled in his shoes, like they were reaching out with all their nerve endings to grip the slippery rainspout through his sneakers. His shoulder and leg muscles burned and he wanted to rest, but his sweaty palms slipped down the spout if they stayed in one place too long. He had to keep going. Up up up.

He was on the roof before Amy had even circled to the third story.

Dr. Miller sprang from one rooftop to the next and Dan followed him, not looking down as he jumped. He tucked his legs and rolled as he landed so that he didn't hurt himself but also didn't have to slow down, popping from the roll back into a run. He'd cut the distance to Dr. Miller in half.

"You can run, but you can't hide!" he yelled, which was a cheesy line, but he was out of breath and couldn't think of anything cooler to shout. It didn't matter. What mattered was that he caught this treacherous medical miscreant.

Dr. Miller glanced over his shoulder, saw Dan, and swerved to the right, crossing a wooden plank that some workmen had placed as a bridge over the large gap between two buildings. On the other side, he kicked the plank away.

Dan ran to the edge, prepared to jump it, but Amy shouted from behind him. "Stop!"

He stopped short, his sneakers skidding right to the edge. He wobbled and waved his arms for balance, nearly tipping over to the wide street five stories down. He stepped back and put his head between his legs to keep from passing out.

If he'd tried to jump that gap, he'd have definitely come up short and ended up with his guts scrambled on the boulevard below.

The doctor disappeared over the sloped edge of a bright-pink-tiled roof on the other side.

"No, no, no, no, no," Dan muttered to himself. He couldn't let this doctor get away.

The gap between the building Dan was on and the building the doctor had run across was way too wide to jump, and without the long plank as a bridge, the sensible thing to do would be turn around, go down to the street, and run around to the other side.

But that's not what a parkour artist would do, and that's not what Dan was going to do, either.

He peered over the edge. Open shutters below him stuck out from the building at ninety degrees. On the opposite side of the street, diagonally across from where he was, someone had left their shutters half open, too. The shutters were about a foot and a half wide, which meant the gap between them over the street was three feet shorter than the distance between the buildings.

Three feet that might make all the difference in a jump.

The building across the way had a cornice just above the shutters that Dan could easily use to climb up, if he could just get to it.

He took a deep breath and turned around with his back to the street.

"Dan!" Amy shouted. "Don't do it! It's crazy. You'll fall!"

"Don't worry, sis," he told her, and then tried to think of a cool line. "Gravity's an old friend of mine."

He wasn't sure if that was cool or not, but he dropped himself from the edge of the roof and landed with his toes on top of the shutters below, his belly, his face, his palms all pressed flat against the building.

What the heck was he thinking? The shutter was only wide enough for the tips of his toes to perch on, and it swayed with his weight.

He let out three quick breaths and spun himself around, pressing his back against the wall of the building for stability and trying to stop the shutter from moving.

On the street below, Habaneros, as the citizens of Havana called themselves—*like the hot pepper*—went about their business. No one looked up at the boy balanced on the top of a swinging window shutter, for which Dan was glad. He didn't need the distraction of people shouting at him.

He steadied himself, held his arms out to his sides, and walked like a tightrope walker to the edge. His knees wobbled.

He tried to stop himself from breathing, tried to stop his heart from beating, tried to stop anything that would throw off his balance. He pictured acrobats and ninjas and parkour masters, and imagined himself as one of them.

He was a master of gravity, a prince of reflexes, nimble as a cat and twice as clever.

Yeah, right, the nagging voice of doubt in his head told him. *But it's too late to go back now, so jump already.*

He leaped from the shutter he was on to the next one. As he landed, the momentum made it swing and he had to windmill his arms to regain his balance.

"Whoa!" he yelled.

"Dan!" his sister yelled.

Amy had leaned over the edge of the building and was stretching her arms down to catch him, but he was too far below.

"I got this," he reassured her—and himself. The crack in his voice was a little less convincing than the words he said.

He leaped from that shutter to the next and one more without falling. He was standing directly across from the half-open shutter on the other side of the street.

This was the big jump, the no-going-back jump, the you're-going-to-break-every-bone-in-your-body-and-die-in-front-of-your-sister jump.

But every one of those kids in the hospital would die if he didn't jump.

It wasn't a hard choice. He bent his knees and leaped, throwing himself forward, stretching out his arms and catching the bright blue shutter across the way with his raw red hands. It stung his fingers when he caught it, and it swiveled open with the force of his jump, slamming into the wall and smashing his fingertips purple, nearly knocking him off.

He'd never be a professional piano player or a hand model, but he held on, in spite of the tears that filled his eyes.

After the pain subsided, he hoisted himself up and sprang to the cornice. His arms felt like jelly. *I'm not going to make it.* He hung there for how long he didn't know, until he heard his cousin Ham's voice in his head.

Muscle is in the mind. If you can think it, you can bring it.

Come on, Dan! he told himself. *Think it! Bring it!*

With a groan of fiery agony, he did a full body pull-up and rolled himself onto the roof. Lying on his back, he wiped the sweat from his forehead and tried to control his breathing, tried to keep from throwing up.

He told himself never to live by one of Ham's mantras again.

When he finally stood up, Amy was beside him.

"Uh? What? How did you—" He looked around for the stairs, glanced over the edge for a ladder, and then looked back up at Amy.

"Gymnastics," Amy said. "Figured if you could do it, so could I. Let's go get this guy!"

Amy was off after Dr. Miller once more, disappearing over the slope of the tiled roof, while Dan still stood there with his mouth agape.

No matter how much they'd been through together, his sister always had a way of surprising him. Sometimes, it annoyed him to have a big sister who was always on his tail, one-upping him with feats of daring and bravery, but he had to admit he was pretty relieved she'd followed him over the street.

He had no idea what he would have done if he'd caught up to the doctor alone.

He didn't need to worry about it, because they weren't going to catch up with Dr. Miller. Dr. Miller had decided to wait for them.

As soon as Dan came down the other side of the sloping roof, he saw the doctor on the rooftop's edge, where he had Amy in a choke hold.

"Stay back, kid!" the doctor shouted at Dan. "I don't want to hurt anyone, but stay back or I'll toss her right off this roof."

"Oh man," Dan sighed, but held his hands up to show he wasn't armed and wasn't moving. Why did people think Amy could be taken hostage so easily?

"You really shouldn't threaten my sister," he said. "It won't end well . . . for you."

CHAPTER 16

"Who *are* you kids?" Dr. Miller demanded.

His arm dug into Amy's neck and he pushed her closer to the edge of the building, but he sounded afraid. His stance was shifting, his body open. He had no idea how to hold someone hostage. Amy began to think she should write hostage-taker reviews the way newspapers wrote restaurant reviews. She was becoming an expert.

"I'm Amy Cahill and that's my brother, Dan," Amy told him, mustering as much gravitas into her voice as she could. Maybe he knew who they were, and at the mere sound of their names he'd let her go with an apology.

"Is that supposed to mean something to me?" the doctor asked.

No luck there.

"No." Amy sighed. "I suppose it's not. Not to you. But if you let me go, I can explain why we need to talk to you and what we're doing here. You're a doctor. I know you don't want to hurt anyone."

She didn't actually know that, but he kept adjusting his grip on her neck, loosening it, then getting worried and tightening it again. A real bad guy wouldn't have cared how hard he was squeezing her neck.

This was a guy who'd fled to an enemy country rather than work on a killer disease, so maybe he had a conscience. Maybe he was just afraid. History was full of people doing crazy things because they were afraid. She wondered how much violence could have been stopped by people learning to calm down and take a deep breath.

Dr. Miller played such beautiful music that she didn't *want* to break his hands.

But she would if she had to.

"I think we can talk just like this," the doctor said, pulling her closer to the edge.

"Okay," Amy told him, "but stop moving me."

He did as she asked. It was an odd thing to be in a headlock, giving orders to the one keeping you there, but it was turning into an odd evening. The sun had set, and music rose like smoke from the city streets below, drums and guitars and singing. Havana was a city of sounds. It would have been nice to enjoy some of it.

Instead, she had to deal with this rogue doctor. "We know you were involved in experiments with goat pox," she told him.

"I left that life," said the doctor. "I'm a jazz musician now."

"That's kind of a big change," said Dan. "Experimental diseases to experimental music."

"I couldn't live with what I was doing," Dr. Miller said. "We had no business altering the pox samples the way we did. It was madness."

"What did you do?"

"The army was worried about biological weapons," Dr. Miller explained. "We knew our enemies had secret pox programs, and intelligence was worried about a pox virus being used against us as a weapon. So they wanted me and my team to see what was possible, to see what we might have to defend ourselves against."

"Wait," said Dan. "They were afraid of someone making a virus into a weapon so they asked you to make a virus into a weapon?"

"That's how the government works," the doctor said. "I did as I was told. I took the goat pox virus—for which there was no vaccine and no cure—and I transformed it. I used the protein coat and basic genetic structure of goat pox, but then I modified its nucleic acid. I made it a non-zoonotic disease. The only animals it would affect were humans. I made it more contagious to humans than the common cold."

"That's evil," said Dan, which was precisely what Amy was thinking.

"Not if you're a goat," the doctor said. "I made the disease harmless to goats. Goats, cats, dogs . . . they can carry the disease around and never have a single symptom. Once infected, they produce natural antibodies to it. In a sense, I did a great service to the animal kingdom." He let out a bitter laugh.

"Listen, kids," he continued. "I hated myself for what I'd created. I told my superiors it was wrong to work on something so dangerous. Even the smallest amount escaping from our lab would threaten the entire world! I wanted to tell the press what we were working on, but the program was top secret. I'd go to jail for revealing it. I was angry, so I decided to play a joke on them. They told me they wanted a disease that would bring a population 'to its knees.' I gave them a disease that would bring one to its feet."

"You created the dancing virus," Amy confirmed.

"I always called it the beat pox," the doctor said. "Like beatbox? Get it?"

"We get it," said Dan. "You're a real comedian."

"But yes, I created it. I used a seventeenth-century outbreak of dancing as my model."

"Tarantism," Amy said.

"That's right." The doctor nodded. "Tarantism was never explained. I thought I'd make a new virus that would explain an old event. That way, if it was ever discovered, investigators wouldn't necessarily think it was made in a government lab. They might think it was an old disease from Europe that hadn't been seen in a while."

"That's devious," said Dan.

"I'm not proud of it," Dr. Miller replied. "But how do you two know about beat pox—I mean, the dancing virus?"

"Because we've seen it," said Amy.

"You've seen it?" The doctor's grip on Amy loosened. "Where?"

"Here," she said. "In the hospital."

"In the public?" The doctor turned a color Amy could only think of as vomit green. "But that's impossible. All the samples are still at the military lab at USAMRIID. It can't be happening here."

"We both saw it," said Dan. "It's happening. And if we don't get a cure, a lot of people are going to dance themselves to death."

"But . . . no," the doctor spluttered. It was like being on an airplane in a storm and seeing the flight attendants getting nervous. All of Amy's calm evaporated when the doctor who'd made the disease showed how afraid of it he was.

"Okay," she said. "Now *this* is happening." She stomped her foot down on the doctor's, taking him by surprise.

"Ow!" he howled, and Amy swung her arms out, breaking his grip on her, then, pivoting around his body, she kicked him in the back of his knee. As he bent with the blow, *she* grabbed *him* in a headlock.

"This doesn't feel great, does it?" she asked, catching her breath.

"I warned you not to threaten my sister," Dan said casually.

"When did you decide to betray your country?" Amy demanded. "When did you decide to steal the virus?"

"What?" Dr. Miller sounded genuinely confused and also genuinely gasping for air. Amy loosened her grip a little. "I never stole the dancing virus." He coughed. "I quit the project and left the country, gave up medicine! I'm not a monster!"

"But you helped a girl name Sinead Starling steal it! Why?" Amy demanded.

"Steal it? Her?" Dr. Miller sounded shocked. "I don't believe that. She came to see me because she wanted to know about my cure for it. She wanted to—AHH!"

Suddenly, the doctor's hand shot to his backside, where a dart had embedded itself in the seat of his pants. Amy looked across the rooftop and saw the woman in the red dress from the jazz club holding a blowgun to her lips.

With another puff of air, a dart shot from the blowgun and Amy was forced to let go of Dr. Miller as she dove out of the way. The dart hit the doctor in the behind again.

"Argh!" he yelled.

"Dan!" Amy yelled. "Take cover!"

Dan and Amy scrambled across the roof, trying to find somewhere to hide.

A man in a tropical shirt, capri pants, and a pastel-pink fedora stepped up beside the woman. He looked like a Caribbean vacationer, except that he had a silenced Uzi submachine gun aimed in their direction. "Oh, just shoot them already," he told the woman in the red dress.

"No," she said. "Mr. West said the doctor should be taken alive."

"I don't feel so good," Dr. Miller groaned, lying flat on his stomach on the roof. Amy noticed his face had gone from vomit green to ice white. The darts were tipped with some kind of fast-acting poison.

"Well, can I shoot the other two?" the man in the fedora asked.

"They're just kids," the woman told him.

"So I'll have to aim a little better." He raised the submachine gun and pointed it at Amy and Dan. They had no cover. Nowhere to run.

Amy was about fifteen feet from her brother. She wondered if she could make the distance in time, dive on top of him, shield him with her own body. She looked up at him desperately, wishing there was another way, any way for them to get out of this.

Dan, who wasn't much good at offering comfort, seemed to see the intention on her face. He shook his head no. "An Uzi submachine gun is a compact automatic weapon designed for urban warfare," he said. He recited facts at the most ridiculous times.

"Why are you telling me this?" Amy asked.

"It has a rate of fire of six hundred rounds per minute," he said. "It'll cut through you like a hot knife through butter."

"I don't know what to do," she said, and tears welled in her eyes. What a stupid thing to happen, after all she and Dan had been through, to be gunned down by a man in a ridiculous hat. She hated herself for letting this happen. She hated those CIA guys for coming to them with the job, and Sinead for being mixed up in it, and even the rest of her own family for not being there to help.

She exhaled slowly, letting the anger go. She knew it wasn't anyone's fault but the gunman's, and the man they mentioned, Mr. West. If Amy was going to be murdered, she didn't want to die consumed by anger. Anger wouldn't save her. She focused, instead, on love.

She thought about all the things she loved in this world, the thrill of discovery, the joy of her friends and family. Her little brother.

She looked back at Dan, whose eyes were darting from side to side, looking for some way out. He'd never make it to the edge of the roof in time, and there was no other cover.

But she could give him cover! She could charge at these goons, and while they fired at her, Dan could get away. It was a long shot, but it was hope. It was one final act of love, and she had no doubt or fear in her mind. She could do this. She could save Dan.

She pressed her palms into the rooftop, readying herself to spring up. "On my mark, run to the edge," she told Dan.

"What?"

"Just get ready," she said. "And remember: You don't always have to be right to be a leader. Just don't forget who you are."

"Amy, why are you talking like a fortune cookie?" he asked, but his eyes went wide when he saw the determination on her face. "Amy, no. Whatever you think you're doing, just don't do it. You can't . . ."

The man in the fedora leveled his weapon and squinted to aim. Amy bent her knees, ready to charge.

But just then, a large dog let out three quick barks.

Amy wasn't quite sure what she was seeing or why there should be a large brown German shepherd on the roof of a building in Havana, or why that German shepherd attacked the man in the fedora.

The dog jumped and clamped its teeth around the man's wrist, forcing him to drop the weapon, which fired a few stray shots across the roof as it fell.

"People really have to stop dropping guns around us," Dan muttered, crouching.

Then the dog shook the man so ferociously that he fell over. The woman raised her blowgun to fire a dart at the dog, but a voice from a neighboring rooftop shouted a command.

"Flamsteed! Go!"

The dog let go of the man, then leaped for the woman, who waved the blowgun to try to block the dog's attack. It caught her red dress in its teeth and pulled as she backed away. The fabric tore and she shimmied out of range, suddenly wearing a red miniskirt. She ran for the edge of the building, and the man in the fedora jumped to his feet, approaching the dog from behind.

"Flamsteed! *Guard!*" Across the rooftops, Amy saw Ned Starling, Sinead's brother, with hair blazing red in the hot Havana sun, shouting the commands, while his triplet, Ted, stood at his side, his blind eyes shielded behind dark glasses. Flamsteed was Ted's Seeing Eye dog, and it had apparently learned to do a few other things, too.

The dog snarled at the man in the fedora, stalking toward him. The man backed away slowly, until he and the woman were pressed at the edge of the roof.

"Who are you?" Amy yelled at him. "Who do you work for?"

The man looked at her, then looked over his shoulder. He took the hand of the woman in the red skirt.

"Oh no," the woman said.

"Oh yes," the man said, and just as Flamsteed charged, the two of them jumped off the roof.

Flamsteed stood on the roof edge and barked after them, while Amy and Dan rushed over and looked down. The goons had leaped down into the big padded backseat of an old Ford convertible, which sped off.

"I think I need to go to the hospital," Dr. Miller groaned from the ground.

Amy and Dan turned to him.

"I think you do, too," Amy told him. "You've got a lot more questions to answer, and somebody doesn't want you answering them."

"What about those two?" Dan nodded in Ted and Ned's direction as the brothers made their slow way across the rooftops. Ned helped his blind brother navigate, while Ted, it seemed, was whispering comforting words to a grimacing Ned. Ned suffered from debilitating headaches, and Amy could only imagine what havoc the stray gunfire had wreaked on his delicate senses.

"If the two of them are here," Dan said, "you know Sinead can't be far. I bet they know where she is."

"They just saved our lives," Amy told her brother. "Maybe we can hold off interrogating them and just say thank you."

"All those people in the hospital are going to die," Dan said, his face stern. "I don't have time for thank-yous."

"*We*," said Amy. "You meant *we* don't have time."

"Right." Dan shrugged. "That's what I meant."

It pained Amy to see it, but Dan had taken the weight of the world on his narrow shoulders. She knew he'd never have forgiven her for saving him instead of herself, and he'd never forgive Sinead for putting them both in the path of danger. The anger in Dan's eyes told her that he was willing to tear the world apart in order to stop this sickness from spreading, and she wondered how far he'd go. Would he save the world but lose himself in the process?

CHAPTER 17

There were police blockades completely surrounding the hospital, and they couldn't get anywhere near the emergency room in the car Ned and Ted Starling had borrowed, not with Dr. Miller splayed out in the backseat, groaning.

Much to Dan's relief, Amy drove. Ted was blind and Ned's headache had him lying down next to Dr. Miller in the back, covering his eyes with the crook of his arm. The old mint-green Packard was huge and there was still room for Dan, Ted, and Flamsteed in the front seat next to Amy.

Amy.

Dan looked at his sister as she drove slowly through the boulevards of Havana's Centro neighborhood. He'd seen the look on her face on the rooftop. He knew she'd been about to sacrifice herself for him.

It wasn't fair. She shouldn't have to do that. People around Dan always got hurt. He couldn't bear it if he lost Amy, too. What would be the point of saving the world if his sister wasn't in it anymore?

"You okay, Dan?" she asked him, looking away from the road for a second.

"I'm fine," said Dan. "Take a left up here. We'll park nearby."

She nodded, but she obviously knew something was wrong. He'd never been great at hiding his feelings, at least, not his angry ones.

It's not Amy's fault, he told himself. *You'd have done the same for her. You can't be angry at her for something you'd have done, too. The only one you should be angry at is Sinead. She's the reason we're here. She's the reason all this is happening. She's the one who has to answer for it.*

"So," Amy asked. "How do we get back to Dr. Neuman?"

"Remember what the doctor said about making this disease non-zoonotic?" Dan asked. "That it doesn't travel between species anymore. That it only affects humans."

"I remember," said Amy.

"Well," Dan continued, feeling pretty proud of himself for what he thought was another genius Dan Cahill plan. "Flamsteed seems like a pretty well-trained dog."

The dog panted happily in the front seat.

"I trained him to announce the dinner menu in my college dorm," Ted said. "One bark for pizza, two barks for hamburgers, three barks for mystery meat."

"He barked three times when he attacked that guy with the gun," Dan noted. "I'm not sure I like what that says about his view of humans . . . but we can send him into the hospital with a message for Dr. Neuman. We can use his card."

Dan pulled out the card Dr. Neuman had given them and held it up to Flamsteed's nose. The dog sniffed it eagerly. The doctor's scent was all over the card. Flamsteed could sniff his way right to Dr. Neuman. Amy scrawled a note for the doctor on the back of it and tucked the card into the dog's collar.

"I'm telling him where we are, that we have Dr. Miller, that he's been poisoned, and to come quickly," she said.

The doctor groaned again in the backseat.

"Whatever they poisoned him with does not look pleasant," Dan noted.

"If we can't revive him, he won't be able to explain the cure for this virus," Amy said.

Dan looked back at the doctor on the floor of the backseat. His eyes twitched behind his eyelids. He was mumbling something, but they couldn't make out the words.

"We've got no time to waste," Dan said. He made sure his sister heard him say *we*.

Dan opened the car door and pointed toward the hospital.

"Flamsteed! Seek!" Ted commanded, and the dog took off toward the emergency room entrance, dodging past the police blockade and the crowd of worried relatives who'd gathered at the checkpoints looking for their children.

"I sure hope Dr. Miller knows how to cure this thing," Dan said aloud.

"I never got that far," the doctor's voice creaked from the backseat, hardly louder than a whisper. "I quit . . . before . . ."

"You'd made the virus, but you quit before making a cure?" Dan clarified. "Real nice. You're like a little kid who makes a mess of his room and then expects someone else to clean it up."

"You make a mess of your room and expect someone else to clean it up," Amy reminded him.

"They had no interest in a cure," the doctor said. "That is why I quit the program. They only wanted the disease, as a weapon. I could not, in good conscience, continue my work. They would not allow me to resign, either. So I fled to Cuba."

"And then gave your research to terrorists," Dan added.

"I told you I did not!" the doctor groaned. He began to cough and was forced to close his eyes again. He'd broken out in a sweat. Staying awake was costing him great effort. Still, Dan didn't care how tired this scientist was. He needed answers.

"We know you met with Sinead," Dan said.

"Our sister is not a terrorist!" Ted objected. "She's in trouble. That's why we came here. To help her!"

"She is . . . your sister?" the doctor asked.

"Yes," said Ned, sitting up slowly and rubbing the side of his head. "She was working in a laboratory in England, cutting-edge medical research that she refused to talk about. Then she disappeared. A few weeks ago, she sent us a message."

"What message?" Amy wondered.

"She told us to follow you," said Ted.

"She wanted you to stop us?" Dan demanded. Of course that snake Sinead would lure them to Cuba just to sabotage them. He wasn't surprised. He was only surprised that Ted and Ned went along with it. He'd always believed they were decent guys.

Ned shook his head. "She just said to follow you. That was all. She didn't say why."

"So what's she doing, Doctor?" Dan whirled back to the doctor. "What did she talk to you about?"

"She had a lot of questions about epidemics," he said. "How an outbreak might occur. She wanted to know about Cuba's health system. How they might respond to an outbreak of my virus."

"And you told her?"

The doctor groaned again. "It seemed harmless. My virus was secure at USAMRIID. So I explained to her why Cuba was an unlikely place for a major outbreak. They have a very effective quarantine system. Such a controlled society, with a strong dictator . . . they can close off entire neighborhoods and imprison people at will. They have stopped the spread of freedom for over sixty years; they could certainly stop the spread of a virus. And because of their isolation, it would be difficult for a virus to spread off the island."

"So a terrorist attack with a virus wouldn't be effective here?" Dan asked.

"Our sister is *not* a terrorist," Ned objected again.

"It would not be effective," the doctor agreed. "And I must agree with your friends. Sinead Starling is not a terrorist. When I met with her, she worked for a drug company. ShkrellX Pharmaceuticals. She claimed they were developing a cure for my disease."

"Why would a company develop a cure for a disease that only existed in a lab?" Dan wondered, and then it dawned him: The outbreak of the disease in Havana wasn't an attack at all.

It was an experiment.

"They want to know if their cure works or not," Amy said, reaching the same conclusion as Dan.

"So they release a deadly disease just so they can cure it?" Dan shook his head. "That's crazy."

"If your sister was sick with it and there was only one cure, what would you pay to get it to her?" the doctor asked.

"Anything," Dan said without hesitation, remembering her face on the roof when she thought she could save him.

"You see?" said the doctor. "Do you see?"

"They could make a fortune," Dan said.

The doctor passed out from the effort of speaking, small spit bubbles forming on his lips with every strained breath he took. At least he was still breathing.

"Greed," said Dan. "This is all about greed." No matter how complicated the plot, the motivations of evildoers were always so simple: Ambition. Revenge. And the oldest motive of all, greed.

Ted and Ned had gone silent, thinking about what their sister could be doing down here. Dan had seen how sneaky Sinead could be. He could believe she'd be involved with a terrible plot, but not for something as simple as money. It didn't explain why she had lured him and his sister to Havana, or lured her own brothers there, too. There were no good feelings between Dan and Sinead, but she wouldn't haphazardly put Ted and Ned in the path of a deadly virus. She had to have a plan. She was, in a way, just like Dan. She was unrelenting in the pursuit of her goals.

But what could her goal be this time? And how could Dan stop her?

Just then, they heard Flamsteed's bark as he came trotting toward their car, leading a bemused Dr. Neuman behind him.

"Good boy!" Ted praised his dog as he leaped back into the car to nuzzle against his master.

"This is very unconventional," Dr. Neuman said, then noticed Dr. Miller in the backseat. "Don!"

He bent down and checked the doctor's pulse, then looked at his pupils with a flashlight. "I will have to take him back to my home," he said. "I can treat him there."

"Not the hospital?" Amy asked.

"We are overrun." Dr. Neuman sighed. "There has been an outbreak of this virus among my staff. I have a third of the nurses I need."

"How are the earlier patients doing?" Amy asked.

The doctor rubbed his eyes. "We have found a way to hydrate them with squirt guns . . . but their bodies are wearing out. One day, two at the most, until they begin to succumb. And I have worse news . . ."

"Worse?" Dan threw his arms in the air. "How could there be worse news than that?"

"One of my nurses went home before she got ill," he said. "Her family called. She's dancing. And now, three other people in her building are dancing, too."

"So it's spreading," said Amy.

The doctor nodded. "I'm afraid by week's end, nowhere will be safe."

"There's a cure, though!" Ted announced happily. "The doctor told us. My sister and ShkrellX Pharmaceuticals have developed a cure."

Dr. Neuman looked at Ted, eyes narrowed. "How do you know this?"

"Their sister works for ShkrellX," Dan explained.

Dr. Neuman looked over at Ted and Ned. "I see the resemblance," he said. "A girl who looks like them came to see me shortly after you left this evening."

"You saw our sister?" Ted asked. "How is she?"

"*Where* is she?" Dan asked.

"She gave me a suite number at the Hotel Nacional where I could reach her," said Dr. Neuman. "She told me her company was at work developing a cure to help the Cuban people in our time of need. She said it would be ready shortly and she would be happy to provide it, if I would allow them full access to my patients." The doctor laughed bitterly.

"Why is that funny?" Amy wondered. "This could be the solution."

"There were two people with her," the doctor said. "Watching her closely. They claimed to be her 'sales associates,' but it was clear they were guarding her. She could not speak freely in front of them. But she tapped on my desk as she spoke. Morse code, which, of course, I know."

"What'd she say?" Ned asked.

"She tapped on my desk as she spoke about ShkrellX Pharmaceuticals coming to our aid," Dr. Neuman said. "She tapped the same message as she said they would be happy to assist my patients for free and when she said they had a cure. She tapped this."

The doctor tapped on the hood of the car, a pattern of short and long taps.

-· --- -·-· ··- ·-· · ·-·· -·-- ·· -· --·

"She tapped it much harder when she said, *we have a cure*," Dr. Neuman said. He repeated the Morse code message.

-· --- -·-· ··- ·-· · ·-·· -·-- ·· -· --·

"Do you understand?" the doctor asked.

"Yeah," said Dan. He knew Morse code. He loved codes. Morse was such a simple one it was almost boring, just a series of short and long signals that stood in for letters and numbers.

But there was nothing boring about Sinead's message. He could barely keep from shouting as he translated it for the others. "Sinead said, *No cure. Lying.*"

"No cure," Dr. Miller mumbled in his fevered half-sleep. "There is no cure. . . ."

CHAPTER 18

It was a beautiful hotel suite in the finest hotel in Havana, but all the room service croissants in the world couldn't hide the fact that Sinead was a prisoner.

Every time she moved, the goons moved with her; every time she spoke to anyone, the goons watched and listened. They doubted her loyalty; they suspected her of treachery.

They were not wrong.

She was betraying them. It was what she did best.

Sinead Starling had applied to work for ShkrellX over a year ago, in a fever of idealism and inspiration. It was an important job, and she'd gotten so bored sitting around taking Internet classes. ShkrellX was a cutting-edge biomedical company. They designed life-saving drugs for all sorts of rare illnesses, from dengue fever to Ebola. They even made a specialized migraine medicine that eased her brother Ned's pain, although for that one, they charged $850 for a single pill.

As a company employee, she would get them for free. It was one of the many perks.

She'd also earn an amazing salary, ridiculously large for a girl of her age without a college degree, and she would get to do amazing work. She'd be a part of the team fighting some of the most insidious diseases on the face of the Earth. Her job would be saving humanity from destruction every single day.

That was what Mr. West told her when he'd offered her the job. She'd accepted on the spot, sealed the agreement with a handshake. She saw her work for ShkrellX Pharmaceuticals as the surest path to redemption. She'd made mistakes and hurt her friends, but she knew if she could help total strangers around the world, then maybe she could be forgiven. Maybe the Cahills would forgive her.

If she had a time machine, she'd go back and smack herself across the face for being such a fool. If she had a time machine, she'd go back and change a lot of things.

She'd been there nine months before she realized that ShkrellX wasn't interested in curing diseases or helping people. They only wanted to make money.

"Don't worry," Mr. West had reassured her. "You can do good while doing well. Just imagine what all your old friends will think of you when a terrible disease breaks out and you are on the front lines of curing it! Won't that be something to celebrate?"

Of course it would, she'd thought. Dan and Amy saved the world all the time, but what had Sinead ever done? She would forever be a traitor in their eyes, unless she did something amazing. Then Amy and Dan and the others would respect her again.

But ShkrellX had other plans. Curing diseases was time consuming and expensive. But if a disease broke out for which they *already* had a cure, then they could simply make a huge profit.

So they wanted Sinead to steal a certain disease from the military. No one had ever seen this disease in the world, so no one else would have a cure. Once it was unleashed, ShkrellX would cure it and the company would get rich.

At first, Sinead had refused. She said they couldn't do it. She said she wouldn't.

Mr. West didn't care. He told her he'd find someone else to release the virus. When she threatened to tell the press, Mr. West said she would never get the chance.

He would have her killed. Her brothers, too.

Sinead faltered.

She wasn't brave. She wasn't heroic. She wanted to live. She wanted to live long enough to stop them. If she refused, it wouldn't change the company's plan, but it would get her killed.

She decided to go along.

The plan was to start as an isolated outbreak in Havana. Then they'd cure it to demonstrate that they *could* cure it. The Cuban outbreak would scare the rest of the world so badly that they'd pay anything to prevent another one, and Cuba's isolation would make the spread of the disease easy to stop. The company would make billions of dollars.

They had no idea that Sinead had tipped off the Cahills just by taking off her mask.

She'd had no idea at the time that there was no cure yet. When Mr. West made Sinead unleash the virus, ShkrellX scientists were working around the clock to develop a cure, but they hadn't succeeded.

Sinead had lured her cousins into an outbreak. She'd made a terrible mistake, trusted the wrong people, and put everyone's lives in danger. She was a fool, but Amy and Dan would save her. They'd save everyone. They had no other choice.

While she sat in her luxury hotel room overlooking the ocean off the coast of Cuba, waiting for the world to end in an outbreak of fatal dance moves, Amy and Dan were free to move about at will. They would find her lab in England; they would see the research she'd done; they would get it to the Ekat lab in the Bermuda Triangle and make their own cure; they would—

Knock-knock.

Someone was at the hotel room door.

Knock-knock.

The woman in the torn red dress got up to open it.

"You again!" she shouted at the teenage boy standing in front of her, moving to slam the door in his face.

He stuck his foot out and stopped it.

"I need to talk to a friend of mine," said Dan Cahill, holding up a glass vial of clear liquid and stepping into the hotel suite alone. "And you're going to let me."

Dan Cahill sure was brave, but as he waved a vial of deadly virus around in front him, Sinead realized there was a very thin line between brave and reckless. One slip with that vial, and none of them would live out the week.

CHAPTER 19

"What is that?" the woman in front of Dan snarled. Her angry voice was far less pleasant than her singing voice.

Dan twirled the liquid in the vial around in front of her face as he took a bold step forward into the hotel suite. She took a step backward. He let the vial slip a little bit, which made the woman gasp.

"You know exactly what this is," said Dan, sounding as menacing as he could. "Sweat from one of the infected teens in the hospital, and unless you want me to smash this open, you'll back away and let me talk to my old friend Sinead."

The woman looked from Dan's face to the vial, and back to Dan again.

He made his best *don't mess with me I'm not bluffing* face, which he worried might look a lot like a *get out of the way I have to go to the bathroom* face. Either way, it worked and she let him pass. The man in the fedora was no longer wearing his fedora. He had his arm in a sling now. He stood rigid, but his fingers drifted toward the Uzi sitting on a side table.

"Don't even think about it," Dan warned, then ordered the woman to shut the door to the suite. He finally looked at Sinead Starling, perched on the couch in her usual preppy attire. He wanted to charge across the room and shake her, make her apologize for all she'd put them through. He felt a scream in his brain, but he left it there. He had to play it cool.

"Nice place," he said at last.

The Hotel Nacional really was nice. It opened in 1930 and had hosted guests like baseball player Mickey Mantle, boxer Rocky Marciano, and movie stars like Buster Keaton, John Wayne, and Marlon Brando. Winston Churchill had stayed there and so had Ernest Hemingway. During the 1962 Cuban Missile Crisis that Amy had told him about, Fidel Castro set up his command post at the hotel to organize the defense of the island from a US invasion.

It had a rich and storied past, which meant that the Cahills had detailed maps of it in their database. Dan had studied them on his phone during the drive from Dr. Neuman's apartment, where'd they'd left Dr. Miller. Dan had another brilliant plan lined up, but looking Sinead in the face was making him rethink it all. His hands were shaking with what he knew must look to them like fear, but was actually blinding, white-hot rage.

Why shouldn't he just toss this vial at Sinead's feet and curse her to a dancing death just like she'd done to so many others?

Because the liquid in the vial was a fake, for starters. It wasn't full of the dancing virus, but rather, a whole lot of Flamsteed's drool.

"Dan," Sinead said to him, her voice thick with worry. Good. Let her worry. "You shouldn't have taken that vial out in public. The virus is highly contagious."

"You would know," Dan sneered at her. "You unleashed it, didn't you?"

Sinead's mouth tightened. Her eyes darted over his shoulder and he spun just as the two bodyguards took a step toward him. "Don't move!" he yelled, and held up the vial. They froze in place again, and Dan turned back to Sinead. "Did you unleash it?"

Sinead hesitated. *Is she afraid of me or afraid of her bodyguards?* he wondered.

"Yes," she finally said. "I did."

"You lousy snake," Dan growled at her. She was a cold-blooded killer, a ruthless, self-serving monster, and she stood there in front of Dan looking just like the girl he'd always known. It was too bad the lies one told didn't leave permanent marks for all to see. Maybe, he hoped, his words could wound her. "You betrayed our family, you hurt innocent people, and now, you've put the whole world in danger. And for what? Why? Do you have any good reason or are you just plain evil?"

It looked like Sinead was about to cry, which gave Dan some satisfaction. There was a thrill to unleashing all his anger at someone who rightly deserved it. This was what made revenge so tempting, this feeling of righteous power.

He suddenly knew how his grandmother had felt when she ran the family. He suddenly understood the ruthlessness it took, the coldness that leadership demanded. You had to believe yourself better than the ones who you fought against, or else you could never do the things you had to do to defeat them. You had to be the judge and the jury and the executioner.

But then Dan pictured Amy's face just before she meant to run into gunfire for him. *You don't always have to be right to be a leader. Just be yourself*, she'd said.

Dan shook his head. He had to move Sinead into position.

He stepped in her direction as threateningly as he could, holding the vial toward her face.

She backed away, toward the window. A tropical evening breeze blew across the room, and far below, palm trees swayed, making the shadows of the lights around the hotel courtyard bend and dance. The ocean sparkled with starlight.

"I swear, Dan," Sinead pleaded. "I thought we'd have a cure by the time it was unleashed. I didn't want anyone to get hurt. They lied to me. They threatened me. They forced me to do it."

"So you let out a deadly disease with no cure?"

Sinead nodded.

"I know this is ironic to say," Dan told her. "But you make me sick."

A tear trickled down Sinead's cheek. Dan wanted her to cry, but not right now. For the plan to work, he needed her angry. And he had a new idea how to do it. "You know Ted and Ned are in Havana looking for you?" he asked.

She frowned.

"Yeah," said Dan. "You know because you brought them here. It's really too bad, though. I guess they got infected. They won't stop dancing. I'm not sure how long they have left."

"What?" Sinead cried out.

Dan shrugged. "It's your own fault."

"No!" Sinead yelled. Her face had turned nearly as red as her hair.

"Yep," said Dan, and with that, Dan threw the vial at the man in the doorway, where it smashed on the wall by his head.

"Ah!" He ducked and covered his nose and mouth, then dove back into the bedroom. The goons scrambled for the door into the hall to escape, and Dan, at the same time, rushed forward, tackling Sinead around the waist, just like Ham had taught him a proper tackle should go, and he dragged her out the window into the clear night sky.

As they went over the balcony and began to fall toward the hotel courtyard, Dan's watch beeped.

They were out the window right on time, as planned; the only problem was that Amy, who was supposed to catch them, was running late.

CHAPTER 20

Amy peered over the edge of the Hotel Nacional roof and looked straight down to the courtyard. A well-manicured lawn stretched out from the end of the lounge area to the fence that blocked the hotel from the road. Beyond the road was the Malecón promenade at the edge of Havana, and beyond that, the dark ocean.

She breathed the sea-salt air in deep and let the breeze run its fingers through her hair. She could see all of Havana from this height. Flickering lights in the windows of the pastel apartment blocks, palm trees swaying in time to the guitar-playing musicians on folding chairs out front. The 1950s-style bungalows in one direction and the 1750s-style villas in the other. Downtown sat El Capitolio, the former capitol building of Cuba that now housed the Academy of Sciences. It was dramatically lit for evening and looked just like the US Capitol building, with rows of neoclassical columns and grand statuary. Nearby, a military tank sat on a pedestal, celebrating the 1959 revolution.

A glance toward Florida showed her how close the two countries were. She thought she could actually see the glow of Key West against the nighttime clouds, but that had to be a trick of the eyes. She couldn't see ninety miles away, could she?

One infected person on the Florida coast would turn to one hundred in a few hours, and then, when they boarded planes and went back to their homes in Tulsa and Detroit and Dallas and Boston . . . in a few days the disease could spread across the country as fast as a dancing cat video on the Internet.

And from one international airport it could reach all the others. She shuddered, seeing how easily a pandemic could erupt. One sick person, one cough, one unwashed hand . . . the apocalypse wouldn't come with some doomsday device or secret serum. The apocalypse would come silently riding in the DNA of one invisible germ.

A light blinked on the roof of the hospital, a signal to helicopters not to land there, that it was quarantined. A grim reminder of the mission at hand. Amy had work to do; she couldn't let fear paralyze her. She might not be able to save everyone on the planet, but right now she didn't have to. She just had to save her brother.

She checked her watch. Four minutes until Dan would be diving out that window with Sinead, and Amy would have to be on her way down on the rappel line to catch them. She'd done a lot of mountain climbing to conquer her fear of heights. She knew her way around ropes, knots, belay lines, and harnesses. She had the skills she needed for success here, she just had to steel her nerves. What was heroism anyway but the right combination of nerve and skill?

Morality, she thought. *That last part of heroism is doing the right thing, even when it's hard.* Sometimes, though, it was hard to know what the right thing was.

Amy hooked the line up to one of the concrete posts that poked from the roof and looped it through her climbing harness. She checked the extra loops of rope and carabiners to make sure they were attached and secure. She'd only have one chance to get this right, or Sinead and her little brother would be splattered into bits below.

Her phone vibrated in her pocket, and a glance at her watch told her it was Nellie calling from Massachusetts.

"Nellie," she answered. "Sorry I didn't call you earlier. We're doing okay, but we've got a problem down here. We've found Sinead, but there's been an outbreak of the disease. Hundreds infected, more every hour. It's . . . it's bad. . . ."

"Glad you're safe, kiddo," said Nellie. "And I wish I could be down there with you. I've always wanted to see Havana. You know the famous daiquiri was invented there? Ernest Hemingway himself invented it at an Old Havana watering hole called El Floridita."

Amy smiled. She loved hearing the excitement in Nellie's voice when she talked about travel and about the history of food and drink. *It's great*, Amy thought, *to have so many people in my life with such interesting passions.* She was about to say so when Nellie cut her off.

"Sorry, Ames, I'd love to tell you more about the cuisine of Cuba," she said. "But there's no time. I've got a problem up here. Ham, Ian, Cara, and Jonah came back from England early and . . . something strange is happening. They found a secret lab, but someone showed up to destroy it. They got in a fight and . . . well, since they got back, they've been sealed in the secondary garage. They've been—I'm not sure how to describe it . . ."

"Dancing?" Amy asked, and her feet wobbled underneath her. She felt faint, sick to her stomach, her own host of symptoms that were not caused by any germ. This wasn't an abstract disaster happening to strangers anymore. Her friends were infected.

"How long?" she asked urgently. "How long have they been going?"

"Cara said it started on the flight and that they won't stop. Not to eat, not to drink. They're sweating like crazy."

"But Cara's not sick?" Amy felt a glimmer of hope.

"She wasn't a few hours ago," said Nellie. "I sent Saladin in with some water because I figured—"

"Zoonosis," Amy said, with some relief that she and Nellie were on the same page. "You knew that cats probably couldn't catch a human disease."

"That's right," said Nellie. "Cara squirted some of the water into their mouths, but when she gets close, they do this headbanging thing that splashes their sweat everywhere. Jonah and Ham make it look all right, but you have no idea how strange it is to see Ian Kabra headbang. I'd laugh if it weren't so unsettling."

"The sweat is contagious," Amy said. "That's how the virus spreads itself. The virus is in the sweat, and when it flies around as they dance, it gets airborne. If Cara isn't sick yet, she will be soon. I'm sorry, Nellie, but you can't get near any of them."

"I'm looking on the monitors now," said Nellie. "Cara's started to . . . oh no . . ." Nellie's voice caught. Amy heard her swallow hard. "She's doing the macarena . . . that hasn't been in since the nineties . . ."

Amy's heart sank. Four friends exposed; four friends infected.

She pictured Ian, Cara, Ham, and Jonah trapped in the garage, jumping and twirling and head-banging until they dropped. Poor Ian, who treasured nothing more than his dignity, soaked in sweat and spasming all over the place like a toddler in a mosh pit, and it was all Amy's fault. Her and Dan's fault for sending them to England in the first place.

It was up to her and Dan to save them now.

"Nellie," she said. "We will find a cure. I promise you, but we haven't yet. We've found Sinead, though, and we'll—"

Her watch beeped. It was time! She'd been on the phone too long!

At that very moment, she heard Sinead scream as Dan tackled her out the window and they began to hurtle eight stories down.

"I gotta go!" Amy shouted, hanging up with Nellie as she ran back to the edge of the roof.

On the ground, all the tourists sitting in high-backed wicker chairs in the courtyard looked up from their frozen daiquiris and the jazz ensemble that was playing, and they saw Dan and Sinead falling from an eighth-floor balcony.

Amy grabbed her extra rope, exhaled one big breath—letting her fear of heights go with it—and she dove.

The line raced through her loose grip. The pulley wheel on her belt rattled as it bolted through, unspooling from above. She didn't slow herself at all and the air blew her ponytail around her head like a pinwheel.

"Ayi!" someone shouted from their window as she zipped past.

Dan and Sinead were falling faster than she was, and she had to twist around in a dive to gain speed, pointing her head straight down at the con-crete. Dan had spread their bodies out wide, trying to slow their rate of fall.

Amy hit Dan's back with a thud and embraced him and Sinead in a wide hug. She clipped one cara-biner to the harness hidden under Dan's jeans and wrapped the other nylon harness around Sinead, locking them all together.

The ground raced up at them. Five stories left to fall, then four, then three.

"Any time now, sis," Dan said. He twisted around to grab the rope, and Amy used the titanium brake on the belay device to slow their fall. They swung wildly as they fell, and Amy had to kick off the wall every few feet to keep them from smashing into it. Sinead, finally catching on, grabbed the line and helped steady it.

"Ahh!" someone in the courtyard screamed. In the dark, they couldn't see the black ropes. It must have looked like teenagers plummeting from the roof in a bear hug.

Sinead looked at Amy. Their eyes met. They hadn't seen each other in person since Sinead's betrayal.

I'm sorry, Sinead mouthed at Amy.

Amy pursed her lips. She wasn't ready to accept an apology yet, not until they had some answers. Not until they all survived.

Two stories, one story, slower and slower they fell, until they reached the ground gently, landing on their feet and unhooking from the rope.

Dan spread his arms wide and gave a flourishing bow to the shocked hotel guests.

"Thank you! Thank you!" he declared, like a circus performer after a death-defying stunt. A few of the guests calmed down, whispered to each other, and then applauded, figuring the show was just part of the hotel's charm.

"I can't . . . I can't believe you . . . you threw me out a window. . . ." Sinead gasped at Dan.

"Really?" Dan said. "*You* can't believe that? Of all the things that have happened, *that's* the one you can't believe?"

Sinead's mouth hung open. "Dan . . . Amy . . . I'm sorry . . . about all of this. But I'm really glad you came. You're the only ones who can help. That's why I brought you here."

"*You* brought *us*?" Dan scoffed. "If you run an instant replay, I think you'll notice I just tackled you out a window and abducted you from your bodyguards."

"I *needed* you to do that," said Sinead. "You're the only ones who can stop this virus."

"We'll get to all that, but first, we have to get out of here." Amy noticed two burly men with earpieces coiling into their linen guayaberas rising from a small table and coming toward them. "Let's go. Calmly but quickly. Ted and Ned are waiting in the car out front."

"My brothers are *here*?" Sinead asked. She gave Dan a puzzled look. "But aren't they sick?"

"Sorry." Dan shrugged but obviously didn't mean it. "I lied. But Ted might be a better driver than Ned, and he's blind, so it's best if we get back to the car fast."

They strolled through the grand archway that led into the vast lobby of the hotel, trying to look casual. Long corridors stretched in either direction, dark wood with black-and-white photos from the storied history of the hotel and of the Cuban Revolution hanging on the walls. There was a museum-like hush inside, the kind of quiet that suggested informants lurking in high-backed chairs, spies watching from the reception desk, and microphones hidden in every potted plant. Amy was reminded of the sword-wielding eye, the police state in which they were operating. The fancy hotel was surely monitored by the Cuban government, which meant it was also monitored by the CIA, and who knew how many other intelligence agencies from around the world?

She spoke in a whisper as they walked.

"There's something else you need to know," Amy told Dan. "Nellie called. The team we sent over to England is back."

She was careful to say *we*. She knew Dan had a way of blaming himself when things went wrong. She wanted him to know he wasn't alone in his responsibility. She was his big sister; she'd led the family before; and she would never let her little brother down. They were a team. They were, and would always be, a *we*.

"What'd they find?" he asked her.

"They found your lab," Amy said to Sinead, her voice as hard as steel. "Clever to build it in the same town where the smallpox vaccine was discovered."

"I was working on a cure," Sinead explained. "Not a weapon."

"Save it," Amy snapped at her. "While they were there, someone else showed up to destroy it. In the process, Ian, Jonah, Ham, and Cara were infected. They're all back in Attleboro, quarantined in the garage, and the boys have been dancing for almost half a day without food or very much water."

"Oh no." Sinead covered her mouth with her hands. Her eyes were damp again. "I'm so sorry. I didn't think ShkrellX agents would be there so fast. I didn't think anyone would be exposed." She looked at the floor, contrite. "Not any of you, anyway . . ."

"I'm sure that's a comfort to all the parents of those kids at the hospital here," Amy told her. "You thought they were expendable, just not us or your brothers."

"No!" Sinead objected, her voice rising and echoing off the vaulted ceilings. "I knew if you came, we'd be able to find the cure. I had to get you involved, do you understand? I needed the Cahills to help me."

"To clean up your mess," Dan said.

"They were going to *kill* me, Amy," Sinead pleaded. "I needed you to get me out. I'm not like you guys. I'm not brave. I'm not heroic, okay? I admit it! I didn't know what to do, so I brought you into this to save me."

Sinead was crying now. Her cheeks were flushed and damp.

"To save you," Dan grumbled. "Of course it was always about you."

"I knew if you came after me," she said, "we could cure this disease together."

"How?" Amy stopped. "How can we do what your little multibillion-dollar drug company couldn't?"

"Because we'll take Dr. Miller to the Ekat lab in the Bermuda Triangle," said Sinead. "And we'll make a cure for the disease there ourselves. It's more high-tech than anything in Cuba or the United States. Dr. Miller will know how to do it; we just have to get him there."

Amy hesitated. She stopped walking. Could it be another trap that Sinead was leading them into, or was this real? Was she really trying to save people or just trying to get away herself?

Dan's fists were balled. He had obviously made up his mind. He didn't trust Sinead and he didn't forgive her. Amy looked at a photo on the wall near the door of the hotel, a picture of Fidel Castro and his commanders during the Cuban Missile Crisis, plotting strategy in this very lobby. This was the spot where these men nearly brought the world to annihilation, all because they didn't trust each other.

Amy made a decision right then.

She didn't know if it was right or wrong, but she was going to choose trust. She would trust Sinead to do the right thing.

"We'll do it," she said.

"But—" Dan began, although Amy stopped him.

"Dan, this is our only way to help the others. This is our only chance."

Dan took a deep breath in and let it out. He didn't trust Sinead, but Amy hoped her word could still sway him.

"Fine," Dan said at last. "But the Ekat base in the Bermuda Triangle is closed up. Abandoned."

"It has its own geothermal generators," said Sinead. "It should still be operational, just waiting for some Cahills to come back and get it running again."

They stepped outside and the mint-green Packard pulled up, lurching to a stop in front of the hotel.

Ted, blind Ted, was in the driver's seat, while Ned, head in hands, told him what to do. Ned appeared to be having one of his migraines. It was not ideal timing, because just then, the two goons came barreling through the lobby with a Cuban policeman in tow, gun drawn.

"Go!" Amy shouted, shoving Dan and Sinead into the backseat. "Drive straight!"

Ted peeled out of the driveway of the hotel as Amy screamed directions at him.

The ShkrellX goons jumped into a modern sedan behind them, and the police screeched off in their own car, sirens blaring.

"Left!" Amy shouted. "Now, hard right!"

Ted obeyed, Flamsteed panted, and Ned groaned in the passenger seat.

"This is a first," Dan said. "A car chase with a blind driver."

CHAPTER 21

"Weave, thirty degrees left!" Amy yelled.

"Watch out! Motorcycle at two o'clock!" Dan shouted.

"Go faster, they're gaining on us!" Sinead added.

"Ahh!" Ned cried, gripping his head with every shout.

"One person at a time, please!" Ted pleaded, sweat glistening on his forehead. "I'm blind and I don't need to go deaf, too."

Dan clamped his mouth shut. He was the only one in the car who was too young to drive, so his advice probably wasn't wanted. At the same time, he really didn't want to die in a fiery car wreck.

"Amy, can you climb over and take the wheel?" he asked his sister.

"Yeah—I—TURN RIGHT!" she yelled as they nearly slammed into the back of a delivery van. The swerve knocked Amy onto the floor of the passenger seat. Sinead tried to move up to take the wheel from her brother, but the sedan behind them rammed their bumper, forcing them to fishtail and knocking her down as well.

Dan was the only one still looking at the road. He'd played enough racing video games to know what needed to happen now. And he was the only one in the car with a street map of Havana memorized.

It wasn't really underage driving if you were just shouting directions, was it?

"Make a U-turn on my mark," he told Ted. "In three, two, one—mark!"

Ted spun the wheel and the car turned hard, hitting the curb, bouncing over it, and finding the road again, then speeding past the police car and the sedan headed in the other direction down the wide boulevard. Dan's stomach leaped up into his throat. He'd left his heart somewhere on the road behind them, but they'd survived. He shimmied forward so he could speak directly to Ted and not have to shout over the tangle of his sister's limbs. The street they were on led right into the fast-moving seaside highway along the Malecón.

"Right!" Dan called when they reached it, and Ted turned them right. They joined three lanes of traffic and zoomed along the coast toward the downtown Old Havana district, streetlights slashing past the windshield. Ned groaned in agony.

Traffic was light and Dan allowed himself to breathe again. "Just keep the wheel steady for a minute," he said.

The road was smooth and straight enough that Amy finally managed to climb over the front seat and take the wheel. Ted collapsed in relief onto his brother beside him. Sinead leaned forward and hugged them both. Dan watched the reunion with a frown. It didn't seem right that Sinead could be so careless with other people's lives but still love her brothers so much. Did loving them make her less of a villain, or did loving them and still being a traitor make her more of one? Dan couldn't decide.

"I'm so happy to see you two," she cried. "I'm so glad you're safe."

"We're far from safe," Dan corrected Sinead. "We're still being chased."

Amy accelerated and wove through the light traffic. Two police cars were back on their tail, and the sedan with the ShkrellX enforcers had caught up to them, too. They zoomed past the decayed colonnades of the seaside buildings eaten away by decades of salt water and ocean winds in a country that had no money to restore them. There was an empty lot where a building had collapsed, and then a tall blue apartment building where the road turned.

Just after the turn, there was a smaller street. "Pull in!" Dan yelled.

The car swerved.

"Easier to lose them in the narrow streets," Dan said with what he hoped was enough confidence so that no one would notice he was winging it. He'd never been the backseat driver in a car chase before. Crumbled houses and graffiti-covered walls lined either side of them, and just past that, there were more apartment buildings, freshly painted in vibrant pinks and blues. Families sat in folding chairs while their kids played baseball in the street.

Amy honked frantically and the kids dove out of the way.

Amy turned again, knocking Dan into the car door with a hard thud, and knocking Flamsteed onto him.

They whipped around the corners, turned and doubled back, and soon the sound of sirens faded away. Amy idled the car.

"I think we lost them," she said.

The engine rumbled while they waited.

"We can't stay here," Dan told her, noticing three shirtless old men playing dominoes down the block behind them. They were looking at the car, and one of the men stood to go inside the building. Over the door was the stenciled symbol of the eye waving its sword with the letters *CDR* beside it.

"Informants," Sinead said. "Every CDR block captain has a radio to report suspicious activity, and you can be sure they're sending a message about us."

One of the great things about being such a young leader, Dan had found, was that no one in most of the world paid any attention to teenagers. They could run massive art heists or sting operations and then blend easily into a crowd, but here, there was no blending in, no going unnoticed. Everyone was watching one another all the time. It made his skin prickle. It was like the whole city was one giant eyeball, judging, waiting for you to get in trouble.

"We have to ditch this car somewhere," Dan said. "If there's a CDR post on every block, they're bound to catch up to us eventually. Those guys probably shared the make and model of this one over their radio."

Amy pulled back onto the streets, weaving around cars, taking turn after turn after turn. Dan started to feel carsick. It would not be a good image for their leader to puke his guts out. He stuck his face out the window to breathe the cool night air of the ocean. Flamsteed stuck his dog face out next to Dan's and panted gleefully.

"Where can we go?" Ned asked. "It's not like five American teenagers and a service dog can just wander the streets of Havana without being noticed."

"We head back to Dr. Neuman's apartment," Amy explained. "He's a powerful man and he's still a Cahill. It's time he served the family and helped us get off this island."

"We have to take Dr. Miller with us to the Ekat base," said Sinead. "He's the only one who can find a cure for this dancing virus."

"Who says *you're* going with us to the Ekat base?" Dan said. "Maybe you should stay here and face what you've done?"

They passed a corner where three people were dancing and a police officer was trying to steer them into an ambulance. Their dancing was frantic and there was no music. One of the dancers splashed the police officer with her sweat as she did a dab, which looked a lot like she was sneezing into the crook of her elbow.

The police officer stumbled back and wiped his face with his bare hand. That was all it took. He'd surely be infected now.

"Don't stop until we get to Dr. Neuman's," Dan said. "It's spreading and nowhere else is safe." He then glared at Sinead. "We should turn you in to the CIA," he said. "Or the Cuban secret police. I wonder how they'd treat the girl responsible for unleashing this virus?"

"You wouldn't do that," Sinead said, but the panic on her face suggested she wasn't so sure. "I made mistakes. I'm not a bad person," she pleaded. "You're the good guys. . . . That's why I needed you here. If someone has a problem, if no one else can help, and if they can find you, maybe they can—"

"Don't quote the A-Team motto at me!" Dan snapped at her. "I'm the only one who gets to quote the A-Team motto here! I'm the good guy!"

The blood had rushed to Dan's head, and he could feel himself shaking with anger. He had his fists clenched again. Amy had taken her eyes off the road to stare at him. He imagined himself through her eyes and it didn't look good, shouting about being the good guy while threatening a crying person. Sinead was making him forget himself.

He took a breath and counted to three. "You've just got this whole thing thought through, don't you?" Dan said. "You're the puppet master and we're supposed to be your little puppets, doing whatever it is you want us to do."

"You're not my puppets," Sinead sniffled. "You're Dan and Amy Cahill . . . and the world is counting on you."

Dan narrowed his eyes at her. She was right, of course, but he wasn't going to admit it. He wasn't sure if her tears were real or just to manipulate him. He wasn't sure if they were still being used in some plan of hers he couldn't yet see, but the fact was, the outbreak was spreading, and getting Dr. Miller to the lab on the Ekat base was their best hope of curing the disease before it wiped out most of the world.

"You'll come with us to the base," he said at last, and Sinead nodded.

"I'm going to call Nellie," Amy told them. "She's got her pilot's license, and I'm going to see if she can safely get Cara, Ian, Ham, and Jonah on the private plane to meet us."

"Even if you can get them onto a sealed and sterile part of the plane, they're carrying a contagious virus," Ned said. "No country in the world is going to let them in."

"Well, it's a good thing we're not going to any country in the world," Dan said. "We're going to the Bermuda Triangle."

CHAPTER 22

"They escaped?" Mr. West asked, clearing his throat.

"Yes," said the woman who used to be in a red dress but had changed into a black tracksuit. It was far more comfortable assassin-wear. She had her blowgun and poison darts in a clarinet case at her feet. "I don't understand why you called us off. We had bribed the police. We were minutes away from bringing those brats in."

Her partner sat beside her on the sofa, rubbing his arm where the dog had bitten him. "Dead or alive," he added.

"Ahem." Mr. West cleaned his glasses. "It doesn't matter. I didn't want you to bring them in."

"What?" the woman said. "But you sent us after them!"

He did not like her tone. He paid her to do a job, not to question his plans, and it annoyed him that he was expected to explain himself.

"Sinead Starling is still trying to develop her own cure to our disease, which would cut us out of this deal. She is suffering pangs of conscience," he explained. "We destroyed her lab in England and nearly neutralized Dr. Miller, whose help she hoped to enlist. Thanks to your bumbling on the rooftops, we failed." He glared at the man. Really, how hard could it have been to shoot a bunch of children with an Uzi? Mr. West knew he should have hired better henchpeople. But he'd wanted to save money, and these two were ruthless and inexpensive. Still, he regretted the choice. Discount assassins were no bargain after all.

"We've invested millions of dollars in curing this virus, and we are no closer now than we were three months ago. The virus is spreading, making the Cubans more desperate with every hour."

The woman glanced nervously at her husband.

"Relax," Mr. West told both of them. "We're safe here. The Cuban government has contained the virus for now. We have some time." He checked his watch. "It's nearing midnight. I imagine the earliest patients will begin to collapse soon. Once the deaths begin, the World Health Organization will panic and offer us whatever we need to finish making our cure. Money will pour in. Then, when we do have the cure, we'll unleash the disease somewhere more populated . . . Boston, perhaps? Manila? Dubai? Maybe all three. They'll come back to us and pay whatever we ask. While the victims dance to our disease, their governments will dance to our bank accounts."

"But we don't actually *have* a cure!" the woman said.

"That might have been true before Sinead reached out to her old friends, Amy and Dan Cahill."

"Are those names supposed to mean something to us?"

"They didn't to me, not at first," Mr. West said. "But I looked into it. They are a very wealthy family, with branches that dominate the fields of arts and industry, technology, politics, and science, including medical science. Our Sinead Starling, it turns out, is a distant relative of Edward Jenner, inventor of vaccines."

"Good for her," the man in the fedora grunted. He didn't have an appreciation for the history of science.

"Good for *us*," Mr. West replied, then cleared his throat, which tickled him constantly because of his allergies. He didn't bother with allergy medicine. He refused to pay the ridiculous prices the drug companies charged. "We'll let them develop the cure, and then, we'll simply steal it."

Mr. West cleared his throat once more and leaned back in his chair. He turned on his computer monitor and watched the little dot that was the tracker he'd placed on Sinead Starling. "They're on the move." He raised an ice-cold daiquiri to his two henchpeople. "To our success," he toasted them. "And to our health."

CHAPTER 23

Dr. Neuman arranged for the Cahill kids to escape by boat in the middle of the night.

"I'm sorry I could not provide more comfortable transportation," he told Amy. "But the government has issued an order to seal the island. They suspect this dancing virus is a biological attack by our enemies, which in a way, it is."

"We appreciate your help," said Amy.

"Long ago, I chose my service to Cuba over my service to the Cahills," he said. "But now it seems I need the Cahills to help Cuba."

"How are the patients?" Sinead asked, looking at the ground.

The doctor took a deep breath. "Their bodies are wearing out. Four of them have collapsed and are on life-support machines now. Four hundred more are in danger within hours and thousands more after that. We do not have enough machines to keep all their hearts beating. When the dying begins, we will not be able to stop it."

"I promise you," Sinead said, "with Dr. Miller's help, we will."

Dr. Neuman ignored her. Dr. Miller had recovered from his poisoning, but he was still quite pale and looked rather seasick, even though they had yet to board the boat.

"Please, take care of my brothers," Sinead said. Ted and Ned, with Flamsteed, were staying behind in Dr. Neuman's apartment. Sinead had wanted to bring them along to get them out of the infected city, but Ned was in no state to travel. Ted insisted on staying by his brother's side.

"We've got nothing to worry about," Ted had told them. "You're going to find a cure."

"I will take care of them," Dr. Neuman told her, finally facing Sinead. "They are my insurance that you return."

As they climbed aboard their small black speedboat along the rocky shore below the seawall, Amy looked back at the island. Up above, spotlights scanned the sky for incoming aircraft. She heard the engines of Cuban military patrols along the coast, but Dr. Neuman assured her he'd made arrangements to keep patrols out of the area for a while.

"I am leading the medical response to this outbreak," he'd explained. "I told the military that this part of the coast was contaminated and they must stay away until I gave the all-clear. It makes no sense of course, but these coast guard types do not really understand how to battle an infectious disease. They do, however, understand orders, and they will follow mine."

Amy didn't ask him why so many Cubans fled the island. She knew that not everyone was as committed to the Communist revolution as this doctor and that thousands of people sought freedom and opportunity in America. She kept her mouth shut about it. She didn't want to offend their ally by suggesting his island paradise might be a dictatorship. Instead, she simply thanked him, promised they'd return with a cure, and helped Dr. Miller and Sinead on board.

"Watch out for Sinead," Dan whispered to Amy as they untied the ropes and shoved off. "I don't know what she's up to, but she's like old sushi. Even when she seems fine, one way or another, she's gonna come out wrong."

Amy was tempted to laugh at her brother's loyalty to vomit metaphors, but there was nothing funny about his mistrust.

Then again, Amy thought, *why am I so eager to trust her?*

She watched Sinead and Dr. Miller secure the samples of the virus they'd collected from the victims at the hospital, while Dan started the boat's engines. Amy glanced at the storage cooler and felt her heartbeat quicken. She was about to head out into the open ocean on a small speedboat with a disgraced virologist, a girl no one trusted, and enough deadly virus on board to wipe out half the population of the world.

And she was letting her little brother drive.

There were four powerful Honda outboard

engines mounted on the back, and they had been modified to run quietly. Dan waited until they had moved about a hundred yards offshore before he looked back over his shoulder and told them all to sit down and hold on tight.

Then he gunned the engines and nearly sent Amy flying off the stern.

She grabbed on to the metal cleats along the edge of the boat and worked her way up to the wheel, where Dan was standing, driving them straight into the oncoming waves and cutting through the rolling swells. The boat rose sickeningly high off the crest of a wave, the engines screeching in the open air, before they slammed back into the water and burst forward in a rush of salt spray and fumes.

Dan grinned from ear to ear.

He hit the next wave just as hard, smacking Amy's chin into her chest. The cooler full of virus rattled in its nylon straps.

"Be careful!" Amy shouted at Dan over the engine noise. "If any of those vials breaks open, we'll be the first kids ever to drown while dancing."

Dan slowed the engines.

Amy turned to look back at the coast of Cuba. Cars zoomed along the coast road, and the red warning light blinked on the top of the hospital. Patrol boats zigzagged over the water with their running lights glowing. The speedboat was black and had no running lights, so she was fairly sure they were invisible on the water. Clouds covered the moon, which certainly helped, and Amy breathed a little easier with every minute they put between themselves and the Cuban coast. Once they were a few miles out, they'd be safe in international waters.

She even started to relax a little and enjoy the high-speed boat ride over the warm Caribbean water.

Her relaxation ended when a spotlight shot from the sky and bathed their boat in bright white light. They hadn't heard the helicopter closing in. It, too, had been running quiet and dark.

"Halt. You are in violation of quarantine. Turn the boat around and surrender to the Marina de Guerra Revolucionaria immediately."

The message was in English, so the helicopter crew obviously knew who they were after.

"Dan!" Amy shouted. "Maybe it's okay to speed up again for a bit!"

"On it!" Dan replied, gunning the engines and turning the boat hard.

Amy lost her footing and fell into the gunwale, bumping her knee painfully. The helicopter turned with them and closed in.

"Halt. You are in violation of quarantine. Turn the boat around and surrender to the Marina de Guerra Revolucionaria immediately," they repeated.

Then the helicopter fired a string of warning shots from the side-mounted machine gun. The tracer fire streaked orange over their heads, and even though the shots were at least ten feet high, Amy ducked. A line of bullet impacts kicked up the water to their left.

"Go right!" Amy yelled.

"On a boat, right is called *starboard*," Dan yelled back, turning right all the same. "Left is called *port*."

"We don't need a lesson in nautical terms right now!" Amy yelled back. "We need to lose this chopper!"

The machine gun unloaded another string of warning shots, this time cutting right across the front—or *bow* in nautical terms—of the boat.

Dan was forced to turn and slow at the same time. Sinead hugged the cooler to keep it in place and to shield it from gunfire with her body. Dan noticed but turned quickly back to steering, and Amy couldn't tell if he was impressed by her selflessness or worried by her closeness to all those vials.

The boat rolled with a wave and they lost momentum, slowing to nearly a full stop. The helicopter flew over them, then spun around and found them in its spotlight once more. Sinead stood and lifted up her seat, pulling out the emergency kit. She took out the flare gun.

"Sinead," Amy warned. "Don't do it! We can't fire on the Cuban Navy!"

But Sinead raised the flare gun and fired anyway. The bright green light streaked across the distance, arcing straight up to the helicopter and straight into its open side door. The flare burst in an explosion of green sparks and the shouts of the gunner and the spotlight operator roared over the sound of its spinning blades.

The helicopter tilted perilously sideways and began to plummet. Amy's heart jumped into her throat. Had Sinead just murdered the Cuban crew, whose only crime was doing their jobs? *Maybe Dan is right. Maybe Sinead is a monster.*

The chopper righted itself and spun around, turning rapidly toward shore. Amy exhaled with relief for the lives of the Cubans onboard, and then she whirled on Sinead.

"How dare you shoot when I told you not to!" she yelled.

"I was keeping us from getting killed!" Sinead yelled back.

"You'll forgive me if I don't send you a thank-you note!" Amy grunted.

"Hey!" Dan interrupted their argument. "There'll be plenty of time to yell at Sinead later," he said. "Right now, hold on tight, because we have to motor!"

Three boats from the Cuban Navy were racing toward them across the water, sirens twirling and spotlights shining. They were still out of range, and Amy grabbed on to a seat as Dan spun the wheel and opened the throttle.

Amy checked the chart that Dr. Neuman had drawn up for them, and Dan set a heading straight along the latitude line called the Tropic of Cancer.

The boat the doctor had provided was designed to be fast and efficient.

"It'll take us about twenty hours to reach the coordinates for the Ekat base," Dan said.

Amy checked to make sure that Dr. Neuman had supplied enough fuel and water for the long journey. She hoped Dr. Neuman could keep his patients alive that long.

"No bathroom on board," Dan noted as he took a gulp from one of the water bottles.

"We'll hold it," Amy replied, and gave Dan a withering stare. "*All* of us."

She knew her brother well enough to know that peeing off the side of a speedboat was just the sort of thing he'd be delighted to try.

Not on her watch, though.

Dan shook his head at Amy. "Killjoy," he grumbled, and adjusted the throttle to gain a little more speed.

Dr. Miller had gone to lie down below in the cabin. He was still weak from the poison, and they'd need him rested when they got to the Ekat base. It wasn't a comforting thought that a disgraced military doctor turned jazz musician in need of a nap held the fate of the world in his hands.

"Only seven hundred ninety-seven miles to go!" Dan announced.

They bounced and splashed through the dark water of the Atlantic Ocean toward the unknown of the Bermuda Triangle. Amy hoped they'd find the salvation they needed when they got there, but she couldn't help but think of the ships and planes that had been lost on this very route before.

The *Cyclops*, lost in 1918 with 306 crew who were never found. The *SS Cotopaxi* lost in 1925, the *Proteus* and *Nereus* in 1941, the *Marine Sulphur Queen* in 1963, *El Faro* in 2015.

And those were just some of the ships. There were airplanes, too, dozens of them . . . crashed, vanished, and never recovered.

Amy knew what had become of most of them. The Ekat base had a large arsenal of ship-killer torpedoes, undersea mines, and—family rumor had it—a pod of trained attack dolphins. No outsider had ever infiltrated the base and returned to tell the tale.

Would a group of teenagers led by a fourteen-year-old who was still pouting because he couldn't pee off a speedboat really be the first?

CHAPTER 24

Somewhere in the Atlantic Ocean

They took turns captaining all night and into the next day, and the next night again. Dan slept when Amy drove, but when Sinead was at the wheel, he did his best to stay awake and watch. He even used the compass app on his phone to make sure she stayed on course. He trusted Sinead about as much as he liked Sinead, and to be clear, he didn't like her at all.

She was lucky he didn't tie her up in the boat's cargo hold.

Not that he could. He was pretty sure Sinead would beat him up if he tried.

He could tell she was torturing herself about everything, but her guilty conscience didn't make Dan want to forgive her. She *should* feel guilty. She was guilty.

He couldn't wait until it was his turn at the wheel again. He didn't have to think about all this stuff when he was pushing the boat across the ocean. He liked to see how fast he could get it to go, skipping over the troughs between sea swells like a stone over calm lake water. He made it up to fifty knots at one point but had to slow down and shut off the engine so they could refuel. Going faster used more gas, but the moment they finished topping off the tank, he opened the throttle and gunned it again. He figured he could shave at least an hour off their travel time, maybe two.

It wasn't just for fun, either. Every hour they saved might save another life. The clock wasn't marking the passage of time. It was a countdown to when the people in Cuba started dying.

And maybe, to when Ham, Jonah, Ian, and Cara started dying, too.

He accelerated again.

He looked up at the stars and took out his phone, pointing it to the constellations. He had an app that told him where every constellation was and overlaid the lines so you could really see what they looked like, an interstellar connect-the-dots.

He found the Big Dipper and Ursa Major, then he turned the overlay feature off. He liked to memorize the lines and then imagine them for himself. He didn't want some app doing the work his brain was perfectly capable of doing. Because he loved space so much, he always memorized the constellations that would be visible at any given time wherever he was traveling, so he'd know just where to look. It wasn't so hard. Just a cross-referenced table of longitudes, latitudes, and times that he checked against his book of star charts.

He kind of wished he'd brought his star chart book with him, though, because something didn't look right. Orion's Belt wasn't where it was supposed to be. Neither was the Little Dipper or even the constellation he'd invented for himself, the Beatrice, a collection of beautiful bright stars, bent into a sour frown, like his stingy great-aunt was judging them from beyond the grave.

But all the constellations were wrong.

He checked the compass on the boat. Their heading was right. He checked his phone compass. It showed a different heading, and when he looked back at the boat compass, it had changed, even though he hadn't moved the wheel at all. The app on his phone started to go crazy, showing them going the opposite direction from the boat's compass, then showing them spinning in circles, then turning a hard ninety degrees to the starboard side.

Then it just started to play a track from Jonah Wizard's forthcoming R&B album, *Hot Sauce Love Boss,* which Jonah had insisted Dan listen to before it was released.

"Because you're the boss," Jonah had said. "You're welcome."

Dan shut it off and checked the printed charts. Ink and paper couldn't malfunction and couldn't be hacked. When he'd confirmed they'd drifted from the heading they had been on all night and all day, he woke up Amy.

He checked the star positions, compared them to his charts again, and brought them back to the correct heading, but he had no way to know how long they'd been off course, or where exactly they were at the current moment. Had he been the one to lead them astray? Or was it Sinead? She'd been asleep, but still, maybe she'd manipulated his app or something.

"I think we're in the Bermuda Triangle," he whispered to Amy when she stepped, bleary-eyed, to his side.

"Why are you whispering?" she asked.

"Because I don't want to wake Sinead in case she—oh—" Sinead had woken up, too. She stood behind Amy, looking at the console, and saw the electronic equipment malfunctioning.

"Electrical interference," she said, completely unhelpfully.

"Duh," Dan replied. Amy pinched him on the back.

He never should have trusted the computers and apps to guide them. The Bermuda Triangle was famous for messing with technology. Neither the navy nor any reputable scientist acknowledged that the Bermuda Triangle was real, and the area was only loosely defined by legend, rumor, and crackpot conspiracy theorists.

All of that was, of course, on purpose.

The Ekats had used all their best tricks to keep outsiders from discovering their base. There were devices to jam radar and confuse navigational equipment, scrambling radio signals and blocking satellites. There were automated torpedo bays and sea-to-air missile systems. There was even rumored to be the world's largest fog machine, just to creep out ships that passed too close and to block aerial photography.

The best part of their defense, however, was the raft of misinformation they'd spread over the years. They'd planted false stories in newspapers and books, crazy conspiracy theories on websites and TV shows. By hiding the actual truth in the open, surrounded by all kinds of crazy stories about ghosts, aliens, and time-traveling Nazi experiments, they made sure that no one would take the claims of a secret laboratory run by a branch of the most powerful family in history too seriously. Information could create a fog just as well as vaporized water, mineral oil, and glycerin (which were the basic ingredients in a theatrical fog machine).

The defenses protecting the Ekat base, however, were very real. The base must have been close to be messing with their boat's systems so much. Actual fog started to roll in over the water, a wall of it approaching them fast. In seconds, they went from a beautiful early evening on the Atlantic to a pea-soup sky. The seas grew rougher, and their little boat rocked this way and that.

Dan had the exact coordinates for the base on his phone . . . which he suddenly couldn't access. It just played the opening bars of Jonah's next hit single over and over.

"Baby, I got spice, but I'll treat you nice, I'm whatever you want, just name your price . . . ooo . . . ooo . . . ooo . . ."

Salt water splashed over the sides of their boat, drenching their feet. They rocked nearly vertical and all had to grab on to something to keep from being tossed overboard into the frothing Atlantic. The fog was thick and the seas so choppy that to be tossed overboard was surely a death sentence, even in the life jackets Dan suddenly realized none of them were wearing.

Oops.

"Get your life jackets on," he ordered, and nobody argued with him. Amy got his for him and even put it around his shoulders herself, while he continued to struggle with his phone.

A massive wave splashed over the windshield and soaked them all, knocking them back. Sinead was the first on her feet, and she got to the controls.

"What are you doing?" Dan demanded. "There's no one there! The base was abandoned after the clue hunt. This is the automated defense system."

"I know how to get through!" she said. "I can get us there! You have to trust me!"

"But I *don't* trust you!" Dan yelled back over the roaring ocean.

The boat rocked to the side, nearly tossing Dan into the sea. Amy fell onto the cooler that held the virus samples, and for a moment, they all froze.

"It's okay!" Amy said. "Still secure!"

"Dan, let me do this!" Sinead pleaded.

Dan looked at Amy, who stared back at him and nodded. How could she trust Sinead so easily? How could she put their lives in the hands of this manipulative, lying Starling? How could Amy be so . . . good?

He turned back to Sinead. He still didn't trust her, but he trusted his sister. If she was willing to let Sinead help, then he'd be willing, too.

For now.

"Do it," he said. "Get us there safely."

Sinead nodded her thanks to Amy—not, Dan noticed, to him—then whipped the boat around, picking up the radio at the same time and sending a message, a series of clicks. Morse code. She was sending a message, a series of letters, but they didn't add up to words.

"What are you saying?" he demanded, fighting his way to her side against the rocking of the boat. "What message are you sending?"

"I'm shutting off the system!" Sinead told him. "It works on an old Morse radio code."

Dan was about to snatch the radio out of her hand. He didn't trust her signals, but he hesitated. Deciding to trust someone was a lot harder than it looked. He kept his hands to himself. He forced himself to wait.

They all waited.

A wave rose beside them, rolling through the fog three times as high as their speedboat. It came fast. It was going to capsize them.

"Any time," Dan said.

The wave charged straight at them, fast as a train, its whitecap curling at the crest. He felt their stern pulling down into the wave's trough, and then, just before it swamped them, the wave sank and rocked them gently as it passed underneath, no stronger than a ripple from a pebble dropped into a pond.

The waters calmed and the fog cleared. Their boat's engine started again, and Sinead turned to resume course to the base.

Overhead, they heard the high engine whine of a small aircraft. Dan looked to the horizon in front of them and saw a little plane moving fast in their direction, dropping even faster.

"That's Jonah's plane," Amy noted.

"They're in trouble," Sinead added. "It's the defense system! They're caught in it, too!"

The plane's left wing had dipped and they were flying at a strange angle, losing altitude.

"Help them!" Dan shouted, and Sinead scrambled to pick up the radio handset again, frantically entering her Morse code signal.

She paused.

The plane kept dropping.

"Do it again!" Dan yelled and Sinead did it again, sending her signal over the handset.

As Dan watched helplessly, Jonah's plane made a sudden drop and, with a great splash and an explosion of water that reached into the sky, the plane crashed into the sea.

CHAPTER 25

Somewhere over the Atlantic Ocean

The flight had been difficult before it had even started. Nellie had long had her pilot's license and it had come in handy before, but she'd never had to create a sterile containment environment on board a plane.

She sealed off the cockpit from the cabin with plastic sheets and duct tape, marveling at the fact that duct tape might have been the most useful invention in human history, at least since the invention of fire and the wheel. She marveled that it hadn't, sadly, been invented by a Cahill—one of the few great inventions in history not to have been.

Duct tape was thought of by a factory worker and mother of two boys in the navy named Vesta Stoudt during World War II. She thought that cloth-backed tape would be easier for sailors and soldiers to use in the heat of battle, saving time and saving lives. So she wrote a letter explaining her idea to President Franklin Delano Roosevelt, who *was* a Cahill, in the Lucian branch of the family. He had the good sense to pursue the idea, and duct tape was born.

Nellie thought this type of history was just the sort of thing that Amy would enjoy, and she wished her kiddos were there to tell it to. She could use the company. It was lonely having only Saladin to talk to. The cat was not a great conversationalist. It was also creepy watching Ham, Ian, Cara, and Jonah dance uncontrollably on the security monitors.

Studying her handiwork, Nellie quickly realized she'd sealed the cockpit off so well, she had no way to get in, so she lost precious time dismantling her setup and reassembling it with a complicated opening in the plastic through which she could get in and then reseal it from the other side.

Once that was accomplished, she backed the plane up to the garage, covered herself in surgical gear, duct tape, food safety gloves underneath dish gloves, and cling wrap, then used a lacrosse stick of Ham's to herd the others onto the plane.

They resisted, kicking and writhing, dancing the whole way. Their pleading eyes watched her as she shoved them forward, then jumped back. Shoved and jumped, shoved and jumped. Their sweat splattered across her suit, and she hoped she had enough layers on. She'd never had to improvise a biohazard suit before.

She got them on the plane, sealed their area, then removed her layers carefully, showered, dressed in clean clothes, and boarded the plane herself through her plastic corridor.

The whole process took hours, and when she used the onboard camera to look back into the cabin, the ragged dancers stood in the aisles, arms and legs flailing. Ham was pumping his fist in the air, like the music only he could hear had reached some kind of crescendo. A moment later, his dancing slowed, but didn't stop.

How long could they have left?

Jonah seemed the most natural dancing to his own music, but Ian looked completely out of sorts. His tailored shirt was soaked through and torn open to his belly button. His usually tidy hair was matted down in three different directions, and there was an embarrassing split in the seat of his pants that revealed silk boxer shorts covered in bright yellow cartoon ducks. He was doing an aggressive version of the nae nae, just behind Cara, who'd only recently broken a sweat. She had the longest left of all of them, but if they didn't find a cure at the Ekat base, a few hours wouldn't make a difference. Nellie would be forced to watch her die, too.

Ian did an electric slide down the aisle. There'd be no seat belts on this flight, Nellie figured.

"Don't worry, guys," she said out loud before she ran through her preflight checklist. "We'll get you help. If anyone can stop this, it's Amy and Dan."

"*Prrrrrrr,*" Saladin purred beside her. She'd secured him in his cat carrier, from which he'd immediately escaped to curl up in the copilot's seat. He had a cooler of red snapper on the floor in front of him, personal provisions for the journey to the Bermuda Triangle. Even in crisis, Saladin traveled in style.

Nellie had filed a flight plan for the Turks and Caicos Islands, cruising along the coast, then going wide over the Atlantic to approach the island chain from the east. The flight path took her straight over the coordinates Dan and Amy had sent her for the Ekat base, where she'd planned to drop off the radar and land. When the plane didn't arrive at the destination she'd filed, it would be reported lost at sea, another victim of the Bermuda Triangle, and the location of the Ekat base would remain secure.

She hoped that would only be the *official* story. She hoped that they wouldn't *actually* be lost at sea, but things were suddenly not looking good.

The plane hit turbulence over two hundred miles out and lost radio contact with land at the same time. Her instruments went crazy, compass spinning and altimeter flying wildly up and down without any relationship to her actual altitude. She tried to keep the plane level and on the same heading she'd been on, but every rough jostle and bone-shaking lurch threatened to push her farther and farther off course with no hope of making landfall.

A thick fog rolled in, shrouding the plane, and Nellie's palms grew sweaty on the controls. With malfunctioning instruments and no visibility to guide her, she could be flying upside down straight into the ocean and wouldn't know until it was too late.

She glanced to the cabin monitor and saw that, at least, she wasn't flying upside down. Ham and Jonah were still dancing in the aisles, while Ian had gotten wedged between two seats.

He was flailing to free himself and his feet were dancing in place so fast that they didn't even touch the floor, but he was safe stuck where he was. Another bump of turbulence hit, which sent Ham and Jonah slamming into each other and then into the ceiling of the cabin. Ham's head took most of the impact, which was probably lucky. His skull was the toughest part of him. He could take a hit or two without it causing serious damage.

An alarm suddenly sounded and she saw the proximity detector flashing. Jonah had outfitted his jet with all kinds of security, and this one told her there was an incoming missile.

Someone had fired on the plane!

Nellie hit the "launch countermeasures" switch, which released a packet of explosive shrapnel for the missile to hit instead of the plane, and at the same time, she banked hard left.

Jonah and Ham crashed into the side of the plane; Cara landed on top of them, while Ian stayed wedged right where he was.

The missile detonated off the right side, filling the windows with bright orange light. One of the jet's two engines burst into flames. The flames died quickly in a cloud of black smoke and the engine died with them.

Nellie fought to level the plane, alarms blaring around her.

"Mrrrp?" Saladin said, which Nellie took to mean, *Hey, why don't you keep us from crashing, please? I am*

a cat of a certain age and I would prefer not to take a swim in the cold waters of the Atlantic Ocean.

Or it could have just been gas. Hard to say with Saladin.

If the automated defenses were still active, that meant that Dan and Amy hadn't disabled them. What if they'd been sunk? What if Nellie had lost her kiddos and flown everyone else into certain death?

She fought with her stick to keep the plane aloft, but she was losing altitude. The fog began to clear and she saw the water much closer than she would have preferred. It was getting even closer by the second.

She had to slow for a water landing.

At their current speed, their plane hitting the water would be like doing a belly flop onto a basketball court from the high dive. The small aircraft would break apart on impact, and they'd all be fish food. Another plane lost in the Bermuda Triangle.

One thousand feet and dropping.

She pulled back on the stick, trying to raise the nose cone. The whole craft shuddered.

She raised the flaps, dropping speed, but was still going too fast.

Eight hundred feet. Four thousand feet. Two feet.

What is happening? She was way more than two feet up. The altimeter was malfunctioning. She had no idea how high she was or how fast she was going. She could see small whitecaps on the water, her only reference point.

They were getting larger every second.

Her arms strained. She pulled back as hard as she could. Her one good engine was making a grinding sound, squealing. Saladin's fur stood on end, bristling with terror.

She wished she'd been able to get the kids in the back buckled in. When she crashed, they might not survive the impact even if the plane held together.

"Come on, Nellie!" she yelled at herself. "It's on you now! Do it! Nobody dies today!"

She yelled a barbaric yawp of power and pulled back on the stick with every bit of strength she had. . . . She felt the nose rise. . . . She might do this! They might survive!

The whitecaps of the rough water loomed in front of her.

That was when she lost control.

The alarms stopped blaring, the instruments stopped twirling, and the turbulence stopped altogether.

The wingtips leveled, the nose pulled back, and the sea before her calmed.

Just below the surface, yellow lights of a runway rose from the ocean.

As the runway broke the surface, a wall of water shot up around them, but the plane landed itself as smoothly as if they'd hit perfect pavement. As they landed, the runway dropped below the waves, sealing itself off overhead above her.

The engines died as they glided to a stop on an undersea runway in an undersea hangar in the middle of the Bermuda Triangle.

The large bay doors sealed over them and the water inside drained away.

"I don't know what just happened," Nellie said to her feline copilot, "but keep your wits about you."

"*Mrrrp mrrrp.*" Saladin sighed and stretched out on the seat, which Nellie took to mean *Through thick and thin, though hardships are legion, I shall always remain vigilant in the protection of my family.*

Or he was asking for lunch.

Nellie opened the cooler and gave Saladin a nice thick chunk of red snapper. In the cabin, Hamilton Holt was bruised and a little bloodied but still bopping. Jonah's dancing had slowed, Cara was on the ground doing the worm, and Ian's dance had been reduced to sweaty twitches, wedged as he still was between the seats.

Outside the cockpit, the hangar was dark. Nellie had no idea what would happen next, but whatever it was, it had to happen quickly, because their time was running out.

And that's when she noticed her own left foot tapping to a beat she couldn't hear.

CHAPTER 26

Bermuda Triangle, Coordinates Classified

"You could've told us they didn't crash," Amy said, staring at the plane, which sat, dripping, on the runway.

"I wasn't sure the automatic landing sequence worked," Sinead told her. "I didn't want to get your hopes up in case—"

"In case you killed them all," Dan cut her off.

"Hey!" Sinead replied. "It wouldn't have been me! The base's defenses were on autopilot!"

"But they wouldn't have been coming here if it weren't for you!" Dan yelled back.

"Enough!" Amy cut them both off. Dan could hold a grudge for a long time, which worried Amy. Those sorts of grudges were just the thing that had led to centuries of conflict between the branches of the Cahill family. He was the leader for the year, and he could easily lead the family back into chaos if he didn't control his temper.

"There's no point arguing over this," she told him. "They landed safely. Everyone's fine."

"No, we're not," Nellie's voice carried across the

hangar to them. She'd opened the small window of the cockpit. "I'm so sorry, kiddos," she called over. "You need to stay back. Don't come any closer."

"What?" Amy asked. "Why?"

In the silence that followed Amy got her answer.

"You're infected?" she asked.

"Afraid so," Nellie said. "I'm not sure how long I've got, but I can feel it starting already. My feet won't stop tapping. Every time I try, it feels like my skin is on fire."

"Don't try to stop!" Amy warned her. "If you do, you could have a heart attack."

"Well, that's not great," Nellie said, and Amy's heart broke. Nellie smiled without showing her teeth and her smile looked a little like a wince. Their guardian was doing her best to put on a brave face, but Amy had known her long enough to see that she was scared.

"Look, Nellie," Amy called out. "We're going to help you. You just have to hang on."

"I'll be okay," Nellie said. "But I don't know how long the others have. They don't look good."

Amy could feel Dan tense beside her.

Portholes high in the hangar walls let dim blue light filter through, although the light faded as Amy watched. Pumps hissed and the whole base shuddered slightly. Amy's ears popped. She knew they were descending, but how deep she couldn't be sure. Saladin's head suddenly popped up in the cockpit window and Amy smiled.

"She brought a cat?" Dr. Miller asked, puzzled.

"That's Saladin," Amy explained. "He's family."

"She brought a cat . . ." Dr. Miller repeated, and then smiled.

"Uh . . . I didn't take you for a cat lover," Dan said.

"Send the cat out to us!" Dr. Miller called.

"Of course!" Sinead clapped beside him. "I get it! The cat's antibodies!"

"Care to enlighten the rest of us?" Dan asked.

"Dr. Miller took a virus that didn't infect humans and altered it to infect only humans," Sinead explained. "So if a nonhuman—*like a cat*—was exposed to it, he could be a host without getting infected. Saladin's body would naturally resist the disease. He'd produce antibodies that would fight it off. If we can adapt his own resistance to work on humans . . ."

"Then we can create a cure!" Amy said.

Dr. Miller nodded. "That's the basic idea, although it's far more complicated. I'll need some assistance."

"Let's go find the lab and get started!" Sinead said, practically giddy. "Send Saladin out!" she shouted.

"Hey, watch it!" Dan told her. "You don't give orders here. I still haven't decided what to do with you."

"I saved your lives and the lives of everyone on that plane, and you still don't trust me?" Sinead asked Dan.

"When everyone's actually safe, then we'll see if I trust you," he answered her.

Sinead looked to Amy, seeking an ally. Amy tried to show no emotion. She wanted to trust Sinead, but that didn't mean it was easy, and that didn't mean her brother was wrong.

If any one of them died because of Sinead, Dan's grudge against her would look like kindness beside the rage Amy knew she would unleash.

"Let's get to the lab," she said. "We don't have any more time to waste arguing."

CHAPTER 27

Dan hadn't wanted to take a nap, but found himself waking up from one nonetheless. He wasn't sure how long he'd been asleep, and there was no way to tell from the artificial light in the hallway or the pitch-black ocean outside the porthole windows. His digital watch wasn't working, nor was the phone in his pocket. There were no clocks.

Or shoes, for that matter. Someone had taken Dan's off while he was asleep and covered him with a blanket.

Amy. Had to be. It was just like her to tuck him in when he was trying to save the world.

He padded along the hallway, not bothering to put his shoes back on, and he walked in on his sister talking to the cat.

"So the centrifuge separates out the healthy blood cells from the virus particles?" she asked.

She had her back to the door and stood next to Saladin in a dark room in front of a large window that looked into the containment laboratory.

Saladin looked up at Amy, and Dan held his breath for a fraction of a second as he thought the cat was about to answer. He had a little white bandage wrapped around his back leg, where blood had been drawn.

When Dr. Miller answered over the intercom from the other side of the glass, Dan realized he'd still been half asleep. Saladin was an amazing cat, but not a talking one.

"We have isolated the virus particles from the infected sweat," Dr. Miller explained. His voice was slightly muffled by the hiss of the air in his biohazard suit. Sinead worked alongside him, also in a biohazard suit.

"We are now attempting to isolate the antibodies from Saladin's blood," Sinead said. "We gave him a shot of the virus, which caused him to produce more of his natural antibodies."

"Wait," said Dan. "You gave Saladin the disease?"

"They had to make sure he was infected," Amy explained. "It's harmless to him."

"The protein shell from the goat pox is strong and keeps killing off his antibodies," Sinead added. "Trying to break through the shell with cat antibodies is like trying to chop wood with an ax made out of Jell-O."

"What a weird example," Dan muttered to Amy. "Sinead's never chopped wood in her life."

"Neither have you," Amy replied, which Dan supposed was a valid point. He wasn't the wood-chopping type. Although he did have, somewhere in his collection, an ax head that might've belonged to a member of the lost colony at Roanoke.

"We'll have to bolster the natural defenses Saladin produced with some creative DNA modification," Dr. Miller said. "Luckily, this laboratory has a next-generation phosphorimager and gel scanner that the doctors in Havana and the researchers at USAMRIID—or at ShkrellX—could only dream of."

Dan had no idea what a next-generation phosphorimager was, but he liked the sound of it and he liked watching Dr. Miller breeze past Sinead, leaving her to scurry after him in awe. He couldn't help but notice how eager she was to help, and how she was, so obviously, in over her head.

Maybe she really had been just a pawn. Could he hate her just for being wrong? People made mistakes. You couldn't judge someone *only* by their mistakes. You had to consider what they did after they made a mistake. Sinead had tried to do something to redeem herself with the family, and she'd put the world in grave danger, but now she was trying to fix it. Dan wasn't sure which way the scales should balance.

Why do I have to balance them? he asked himself. Maybe judging Sinead wasn't up to him.

Dr. Miller moved through the lab with speed and efficiency. He looked almost the same as he had on the stage in the jazz club in Havana. His fingers worked the pipettes and syringes the way they had worked the keys on his trumpet. There was no tune this time, and the music he was composing would hopefully bring all the dancing to a stop. Dan didn't know what they were doing in that lab, but he watched it for ages, until finally, the doctor took a syringe and passed it to Sinead.

"Would you please place some of this on one of the infected samples," he said.

Sinead took the syringe and a small glass slide on which she had smeared some of the virus particles they'd separated from the infected sweat back in Havana. She squirted the new concoction onto the slide and set it underneath a microscope.

"Could we see please?" Amy asked over the intercom, and Sinead hit a button. A screen lit up in the observation room, and they could see what was happening on a microscopic level.

"Those are the virus particles there," Dr. Miller said, and Dan recognized the bricklike shape of the goat pox virus. "And these are Saladin's modified antibodies."

It was like watching a slow-motion battle as the new, soccer-ball-shaped particles attached themselves to the oblong brick-shaped particles of the dancing virus. For a while, it wasn't clear that anything was happening. Little specs wiggled around, balls and bricks attached to each other and sort of merged. Dan felt his eyes glazing over with boredom. He'd been mindlessly petting Saladin, who was purring and resting happily on the padded stool.

All of a sudden, Sinead and Dr. Miller cheered. Even Amy was clapping. Dan realized he'd completely spaced out for a long time.

"What?" he asked. "What happened?"

"Look!" his sister said. "Look!"

On the screen, the soccer-ball-shaped particles had devoured all the brick-shaped particles with the thoroughness of Saladin eating a plate of red snapper. There were none left.

"So . . . it's cured?" Dan asked, hopeful.

"We can't say for certain." Dr. Miller dashed his hopes. "We need to test this on a living subject to make sure it works.

"Like a lab rat?" Dan asked, looking around for cages.

"Not a lab rat," Dr. Miller said. "We need to test it on a human subject."

"Fine," said Sinead, without a moment's hesitation. "Test it on me."

"What?" said Amy.

"What?" said Dan.

"I got us all into this mess," Sinead told them. "So test it on me. Infect me with the virus, and then, use this cure on me."

"You would volunteer to be infected?" Dan couldn't believe it.

"Unfortunately," Dr. Miller told her, "the virus takes too long to mature in a host for us to test it on you. We only have a few hours . . . if that. We need a subject currently suffering from the full effects of the disease."

"Someone on the plane," Sinead said sadly.

"Hey, no!" Amy shouted over the intercom. "We're not testing some experimental cure on them! Our friends are not lab rats! What if the cure is worse than the disease?"

"Amy." Dan reached out and took her hand off the intercom button. "It's the only way to save them. If the cure doesn't work, they're doomed anyway. All of us are."

Amy's lip quivered, but she didn't disagree. For a moment, Dan wished he hadn't gotten up from his nap, wished he'd just stayed under the blanket, cozy and safe. But he had a job to do. He pressed the intercom button. "Connect our intercom to the plane's radio," he said.

Sinead typed a few keys on her keyboard, slowly because she had to type with giant biohazard suit fingers, but eventually, she looked up to the window and gave Dan the thumbs-up.

"Nellie," Dan said.

"I'm here, kiddo," Nellie said. "I'm . . . I'm . . ." She was having trouble talking. "I can't sit still. I'm so sorry . . ."

"It's okay," said Dan. "We might have found a cure. We're going to help all of you."

"Oh, that's good n . . . n . . . news," said Nellie. "Ham and Jonah have slowed down. They're just kind of standing and twitching. I gave them all some water, but now . . . well . . . I couldn't aim anymore."

Dan let go of the intercom button. He didn't want Nellie to hear him gasp.

Amy got on the radio. "What about Ian?" she asked.

"Oh, Ames," Nellie said. "He fell. I thought he'd passed out, but it was like the virus wouldn't let him stay down. He hauled himself to his feet and kept dancing. He keeps falling and twitching and getting up again. He can barely move when he's standing. I don't know . . . I don't know how much longer he can go on. I don't know how much longer I—"

The radio went dead.

"Nellie!" Dan shouted. "Nellie, do you copy?"

His hands shook. He looked up at Amy, her own face a mirror image of how he felt. Heartbroken. Terrified.

"We need to test this cure," said Dan. He spoke back to Dr. Miller in the lab. "Can we just send Saladin into the plane with it? If they all breathe it in, will that work?"

"No," said Dr. Miller. "Someone will need to inject it into them." The doctor took a syringe filled with a sample of the cure and inserted it into a gas-powered injection needle, just like the one Dan had used on the smuggler back in Boston. "Someone will need to enter the plane in a protective suit and fire this needle into one of your infected friends. It is not without risk."

"I'll do it!" Amy, Dan, and Sinead said at the exact same time.

"They will resist," Dr. Miller told them. "You may have noticed that the symptoms grow more severe when anyone tries to calm them down. You might be attacked and exposed to the virus yourself as you are trying to provide the cure."

"I'm doing it," Amy said firmly. "I want to do it."

"Amy—" Dan started, but his sister had the look on her face that she always got when her mind was made up. Dan nodded but couldn't find his voice to agree. It was so much harder to let someone you cared about risk their life than it was to risk your own.

But there would be no talking Amy out of it.

"I think I can get Ian to cooperate," she said. "Just get me into a suit and get me on that plane."

CHAPTER 28

The hiss of air in her biohazard suit was louder than she'd thought it would be, drowning out the *thump thump thump* of her heartbeat. Her steps across the hangar slowed as she approached the plane.

Outside, she was safe. Inside, a microscopic killer waited for her.

She paused for a moment by the stairs and looked up toward the cockpit, where Nellie was peering down at her, worry lines carved into her face, her head nodding to a tune only she could hear. Amy gave her a thumbs-up, which Nellie could not return.

"Don't worry," she said inside her suit. "I'm coming for you."

She took the stairs one laborious step at a time toward the cabin door and pushed her way into the dim light of the private jet. She was immediately glad for the air hose and breathing mask she wore. Not only was it keeping her from getting infected, it was keeping her from smelling the inside of the cabin. She'd never imagined a smell could be visible before, but Jonah Wizard's private jet looked like it *stank*.

The fine leather seats were damp from where Nellie had been spraying water to get the others hydrated; the walls were moist with condensation from nearly two days of frantic dancing; and the carpeting squished underfoot, soaked through with sweat. Amy didn't dare think about the lavatory at the back of the plane, although she didn't need to. The infected hadn't been using it anyway.

It took her eyes another moment to fully adjust before she took in the sorry sight of her sick friends. Cara was the nearest to her. She bopped and hopped and shuffled her feet along by the cockpit door, misting the plastic with her breath. Her eyes were wide and her mouth hung open. Her clothes were wrinkled but not yet ruined.

The same could not be said for Jonah, Ham, or Ian.

Jonah looked like he was slow dancing with himself, rocking from side to side with hardly any strength left, but unable to stop. His skin had gone gray, his lips were practically white, and there was no shine in his eyes. When Amy clicked on the flashlight attached to her sleeve, Jonah didn't react. He just swayed, like a zombie, raising and lowering his arms.

He fell and Amy gasped, but he caught himself and kept moving.

Thump thump thump, her heart beat in her chest. Every beat was like a clock counting down.

Beside Jonah, Ham was headbanging. His feet stomped the floor, splashing with every impact, and his head whipped up and down. His sweat had all dried, so his pale skin and blond hair were crusted with salt, and he too had lifeless eyes, their normal ice blue faded to the color of Boston gutter slush. His shirt and his track pants were plastered against him, like he'd been swimming, and the fabric looked as heavy as steel.

But it was Ian who made Amy whimper.

His eyes had sunk into black pits, while his cheeks had drawn inward on his already thin face. His mouth hung open and his gums had turned white. He looked more skeleton than human. His clothes were torn and tattered, soaked, and stained in a way that would have shocked and shamed him if he were at all capable of shock or shame anymore. He'd worn through the soles of his leather shoes and kicked his toes raw trying to escape from behind the seat where the flight had wedged him.

He lurched heavily toward Amy, his arms open, and he spun in a circle. His head hung down and rose up again, as if his neck couldn't hold its weight but was trying to.

He fell.

Instinct thrust her forward to grab him by the elbow and help him up just as his knees hit the floor with a thud that shook the plane. He didn't cry out or even wince, although he'd bloodied himself in the fall. As she tried to help him up, he looked at her, eyebrows furrowed at her face plate and one of his shaking hands resting its sweaty palm across the mask she wore.

Then, as if shocked, he snapped his hand away and threw himself backward, limbs shuddering and resuming his impossible dance. Amy stepped toward him again, then she felt herself pulled back. She whirled and came face-to-face with Hamilton Holt, mad-eyed and grasping. He wasn't his usual self, but he still had some strength in him, enough to keep her from breaking his grip.

"Ham!" she shouted. "I'm here to help! Let go!"

He still held her, swaying back and forth.

He was dancing with her, forcing her to dance. He leaned in, using her to hold himself up. His eyes had a panicked look, and his mouth, opening and shutting soundlessly, seemed to mouth the word *help* over and over again.

Amy tried to break away but she couldn't. He started to headbang again, hitting her face plate hard with his forehead. It twisted but stayed sealed. Another blow came and then another. Her head jostled inside, the plastic bent.

He was going to rupture her suit.

"Ham! Stop it!" she shouted, although she knew he wasn't doing it on purpose. He *couldn't* stop it. The virus was driving him mad. The virus was trying to spread itself, and Amy would be the next infected.

Her arms were pinned to her sides, and she couldn't raise the syringe. She had to get the cure into one of them. She tried to lift it, but it fell from her gloved hands. Ham's dancing feet kicked it away, and it rolled behind her.

"No!" she yelled.

Another blow from his head rattled her vision. The air hissed inside her suit.

"Amy!" Dan's voice came over the radio in her ear. "Amy, you have to get away from him. You're going to be exposed."

"I'm trying, Dan!" she replied. "Ham's not exactly a lightweight, even sick."

Another brain-rattling blow. She feared Hamilton might knock her out before her suit broke. She'd be no good to anyone unconscious.

"I'm coming in to help you," Dan said.

"No!" Amy replied. "I've got this."

"You don't!" Dan said.

"I'll be okay!" Amy yelled, struggling. "Just give me a minute. I don't want you coming in here, Dan."

"Behind you!" Dan yelled so loud it made Amy's ears ring.

She craned her neck around in time to see Ian coming toward her. He walked like a zombie, throwing one leg forward from the hip, then the other. His arms waved like he was at a techno rave, and he reached out to her, grabbing her arm just above where Ham held her. He pulled once, then again. *He's going to tear the suit*, she thought, when suddenly, she broke free of Ham's grip and tumbled away, falling on top of Ian.

Their eyes met through the fog of her face plate.

"Ian," she said. "You're still in there."

He opened his mouth, then closed it again. He let out a long, wheezing breath, loud enough for her to hear over the roar of the air flow in her suit. His eyes began to shut. His twitching slowed. She put a gloved hand against his neck, tried to feel a pulse. It was faint and getting fainter.

"No, no, no, no, no . . ." she said. "I am not losing you!" she yelled, and grabbed for the syringe on the floor under the seat beside her. She pressed it directly against his neck, hit the firing button, and unleashed the cure into him with a loud hiss. His eyes burst open at the shock of the needle, then began to close again. She rolled off him and stood.

Ham was still headbanging, Jonah was still fist pumping, and Cara had begun to twirl faster and faster.

But Ian lay still.

"Is he—" Dan's voice was in her ear again, almost whispering. "Did he—"

Amy bent down to check his pulse again.

"He's alive," she told Dan. She pulled out her canteen and put it directly against his mouth, pouring water in. She had to rub his throat to make him swallow, but he kept it down. She gave him more water. "I'm staying in here to keep him that way."

She expected her brother to argue with her, but he didn't say anything. Perhaps he understood that there would be no talking her out of staying, or perhaps he agreed with her.

She didn't consider the third option, until the new voice spoke in her ear, the voice of a man who began every sentence by clearing his throat.

"Good," said Mr. West. "We'd like to see that the cure works before we take it from you. And if you try anything, we will simply inject your brother with the virus, which is currently in a needle pressed to his neck."

"Oh, Dan." Amy sighed. Being held hostage was quickly becoming a family tradition. She wondered how the ShkrellX people had found them, and then she remembered another unwelcome family tradition: being betrayed.

CHAPTER 29

Thump ba da thump ba da thump ba da thump.

Follow the beat. The beat is your life.

Move to the beat.

Keep moving.

Don't stop moving.

Thump ba da thump ba da thump ba da thump.

But he was so tired. He tried to stop, but stopping was agony.

Ian's muscles burned and his stomach felt like a block of dry ice, somehow burning and frozen at the same time. His mouth felt full of wasps or cotton or taffy, and when he tried to scream, his throat seized. His skin tingled, and every lock of hair on his head was a razor blade in his skull.

But if he danced, the pain quieted.

At first, it had been puzzling, an odd tingling of the limbs, a jitteriness he thought was mere nerves. It had begun on the flight back from England, and he hadn't thought much of it. He was restless, but he figured it was due to his new role as errand boy for Dan Cahill, a minion rather than a leader. It was not a role he relished, and it made him antsy. If the others were antsy themselves, as he had noticed they were, then they had their own reasons.

Jonah began to annoy him. He was the first to start dancing, and Cara was forced to take over flying the plane so that Jonah could do the robot.

Ian had ordered him to stop, but Ham joined in. It was unlike Hamilton Holt to dance in public and certainly unlike him to dance to no music. Their movement was making Ian's stomach ache. His head began to throb.

After an hour of watching them dance like fools over the Atlantic, he'd found himself tapping his own foot along to a beat in his head. His heartbeat had a rhythm to it, too, he'd noticed. It was a kind of song. He'd never considered that before—that one's blood made music as it coursed through one's veins.

The thought made him smile, made him bop his head. And as he moved, his stomach calmed, his headache vanished. He wanted to move. He needed to move. He stood and began to dance, and it felt wonderful.

Thump ba da thump ba da thump ba da thump.

That was the last wonderful feeling he had. Once he'd started, he couldn't stop. Time lost all meaning and his thoughts blurred. He was aware of himself dancing, of course, but the memories were disjointed. He felt himself being ushered from the plane into a car, where he squirmed and writhed to keep moving. His vision had narrowed to a thin point of light, but he didn't mind. He didn't need to see, only to move.

He remembered being in the garage, remembered being thirsty.

The cat was there. Saladin. He remembered picking the cat up, dancing with it until it scratched him and he let go.

He'd kept dancing, but it had started to hurt. He was thirsty and tried to stop to drink the water Cara offered.

Thump ba da thump ba da thump ba da thump.

When he stopped dancing, it felt like his body burst into flames.

He started dancing again. He knew he was sweaty. He knew he was undignified. He knew he was thirsty and tired and wanted only to stop dancing, but could not stop dancing.

The next thing he knew, he saw Amy.

She was in some kind of space suit. It made no sense.

They were on a plane and she was in a space suit and Ham was dancing with her.

What a good idea, Ian had thought. *To dance with someone. To share the beat.*

Thump ba da thump ba da thump ba da thump.

"Amy," he tried to say. "Amy, do you hear? Dance with me!"

But no sound came out. When he tried to shout for her, it was like swallowing glass.

Ham was headbutting her. That stupid heavy-metal dance of his wasn't right. The beat was all wrong. Amy could never dance with him to that. She needed to dance with Ian, to hear Ian's music.

Amy, dance with me! He thought it so loudly that maybe she could hear it, and as he looked at her in her space suit, he saw her face through the mask. It wasn't Amy's face, though. It was his sister, Natalie's. She was here, in the suit. She had come to dance with Ian. She had come back. She wasn't dead. She was here!

Thump ba da thump ba da thump ba da thump.

Ian grabbed her, grabbed at his sister. If he could just dance with her, the pain would stop. If he could just dance with his sister one time, then everything would be okay. He would dance with her now and they would dance forever together.

He pulled at her and felt himself falling. Above him, his sister's face behind the mask smiled at him. He could join her. He could see her again. All he had to do was let go.

"Not yet," she said, which was strange because he heard her so clearly, more clearly than he had ever heard anything in his life. "Not yet," she said again. "No. No, no, no, no, no."

But it wasn't Natalie's voice anymore. It was Amy's. And it was Amy's face above him now, staring through the mask.

And it was Amy pressing something against his neck; Amy jolting him with a thousand bolts of lightning in his veins; and it was Amy's face he saw when he stopped moving.

It was Amy's face above him telling him that he was still alive.

CHAPTER 30

"How did you get in here?" Dan demanded, although his question didn't sound quite as confident as he'd meant it to, because a jazz singer in a black tracksuit had a syringe pressed against his throat.

"Our friend Sinead cleared the path for us," Mr. West told him. "It was very nice of her to shut off the defenses and lead us."

Dan looked around, and Sinead was nowhere to be seen. That treacherous redheaded Starling! She'd slipped away while he was focused on Amy in the plane. Of course it had been a mistake to trust her. Dan should never have let her come! He should have trusted his instincts. He should have trusted his memories. He should have trusted anyone but her. "Lousy, lying . . ." he grumbled, which made Mr. West laugh.

"Don't be too hard on her, kid," he said. "She didn't have much of a choice."

"There's always a choice," said Dan. "Nobody's born a hero or a villain. The things we choose to do make us one or the other. And Sinead always chooses the other."

"Such a—*ahem*—powerful sermon from someone so young," the man said. "Yet you fail to see that not everything is black and white. There are gray areas of morality, and your friend Sinead, like all of us, resides in them. She didn't know we had put a tracking device on her, and she didn't know that when she shut off the defenses to guide you in, she was allowing us to follow behind."

"So . . . you tricked her?" Dan asked.

Mr. West nodded. "She is only guilty of being naive," he said. "As are you, for thinking you could stop us. We have invested far too much in this outbreak to let you give away the cure for free."

"But there are thousands of infected in Havana!" Dan protested. "You'd let them die if they can't pay?"

Mr. West shrugged.

"You're insane," Dan told him.

"Now, Dan—*ahem*." The man cleared his throat. "There is no need to bring mental illness into this. I am not insane. I *want* to share this cure with the world. I *want* to prevent a catastrophe. That I intend to profit by it is beside the point. My company and I serve civilization in our own way, and the money we make will be invested in more research into cures for other diseases."

"Other diseases you manipulate!" Dan hurled the accusation at him. He wished he had something heavier than accusations to hurl. The needle against his neck was pretty sharp, and he'd really have liked to get it off him. He never liked shots.

"You should be grateful," Mr. West said. "If this cure works, we will allow you to distribute it to all your friends . . . for a price. Of course, you'll be wasting your money, as we have set explosives to detonate this entire base with you in it. We can't have witnesses, you understand?"

"What if your cure doesn't work?" Dan asked. "What'll you do then?"

"Let's just hope it works," Mr. West said. Hope was not the answer Dan was hoping for.

Minutes went by, but they felt like hours. No one spoke. They simply waited.

Dan hated waiting.

He was tired of standing there with a needle against his neck. He was tired of everyone he ever met turning out to be a traitor. He was tired of greed and lunacy and violence, and most of all, he was tired of being a hostage.

It was time to end this.

Time for action.

"Can I talk to my sister?" he asked. "To check in?"

Mr. West pressed the radio button. "Don't try . . . *ahem* . . . anything."

"What could I possibly try?" Dan answered him meekly, and he felt the jazz singer tighten her grip on his arm. She didn't appreciate his sarcasm. They all knew there was not a lot he could try. The sharp needle point pushed against the soft skin of his throat and limited his options severely. If the woman so much as sneezed, he'd find himself dosed with the dancing virus.

"Hey, Ames," Dan said, looking at the screen that showed the interior of the plane. His sister looked up toward the camera. She was still leaning over Ian, watching the other three to make sure they didn't attack her again or collapse. They were still dancing, but barely, like old windup toys winding down. He wondered what was happening back in Havana, how much worse things had gotten in the time they'd been gone. "So . . . uh . . . does it look like the cure is working?"

"Hard to say," said Amy. "But Ian's pulse is stronger, and he's not twitching anymore."

"We kind of need a yes or a no up here," Dan said. "It's important."

"I think . . ." Amy checked Ian's pulse again, leaned over, and listened to his breathing. He whispered something in her ear, to which she nodded and squeezed his hand. "Yes!" she declared. "Yes, it's working! It's working! We have to get more of it made right away!"

Mr. West grinned a Cheshire grin. "Wonderful news!" he declared.

"It really is," said Dan. "Because now I feel a lot better about doing this!"

He closed his eyes against the sharp pinprick as he deliberately shoved himself sideways, sticking himself with the needle right in the neck.

"OW!" he yelled, but the shock of the movement knocked the woman away.

She'd never expected him to infect himself on purpose.

He swept her legs out from under her with a low kick as he yanked the syringe out of his neck. "Ow! Ow! Ow!" he shouted, although it hurt less than a tetanus shot did, but he wanted the others to be afraid of that needle. It was his only weapon.

He lunged for the man with the machine gun, who dodged but tripped over Mr. West, who was also diving out of the way.

"Amy, try to start the plane's engine!" Dan yelled before bolting for the hallway into the corridor.

"After him!" Mr. West yelled. "He'll be headed to the lab!"

Dan didn't look back, but he heard the repeated *crack crack crack* of machine-gun fire and sparks ignited off the metal walls around him. Gunfire in a pressurized undersea fortress?

Brilliant.

He ran around the corner and raced for the lab. He hoped they'd be growing more samples of the cure in those petri dishes, because whatever they had by the time he got there was all they were going to have to work with.

Mr. West had set the whole base to explode, and Dan didn't intend to be on it when it did.

Even if he didn't blow up, how long, he wondered, did he have before he started dancing?

CHAPTER 31

Sinead Starling had always done the right thing, until she had started to do the wrong things. And once she'd turned down that path, it seemed like she could never go back.

She'd been a fool to trust ShkrellX and then a fool to lead them straight to the Ekat base. It was all her fault.

But she could make it right.

So yes, she'd taken Dr. Miller hostage in the lab at the point of an air rifle, ordering him to load syringes with as much of the cure to the dancing virus as he had.

"You don't need to point that thing at me," Dr. Miller told her over the radio in his biohazard suit. "I *want* to get this cure to as many people as we can. I'm on your side."

"I've learned not to trust anyone," said Sinead. "So I'll keep pointing it at you all the same."

"You teach people how to treat you, you know?" Dr. Miller said. "If you can't trust anyone, maybe it's because you don't make it easy to trust you?"

"Spare me the talk-show self-help," Sinead answered him, perhaps more venomously than she needed to. He'd struck a nerve. She *wanted* to be trustworthy, and she *wanted* to trust people. But trust took time to build, and she didn't have time.

"Just keep loading those vials," Sinead ordered him. "We're getting out of here with the cure for this virus, whatever it takes."

"It's funny you say *we*," a voice cut into her ear over the radio. It wasn't Dr. Miller's. It was Dan's. "You think you're one of us again?"

She whirled around and saw him standing in front of her, holding a radio handset. He was in the lab but without a protective suit. What was he thinking?

"Dan?" she gasped. "What are you doing in here without a suit on? Are you crazy?"

"Don't worry about me," he replied. "You never have before."

"I didn't betray you this time, I swear," she pleaded with him. "But you need to put a suit on."

"I don't," he told her. "I'm already infected."

Her heart sank. She'd only gotten Dan and Amy involved because ShkrellX wouldn't let her out of their sight. She'd never thought Amy and Dan would end up infected themselves. *I never meant to hurt anyone.*

But what she meant to happen and what actually happened always had a way of being different.

"I never wanted it to happen this way," Sinead told him. "Believe me."

"I know," said Dan. "You got in over your head. But you should have called us when you got in trouble, not lured us with lies and trickery. We would've helped you if you'd asked. That's what *we* do, as a family. We help people who have nowhere else to turn for help . . . if they know how to find us."

"Oh," Dr. Miller interrupted. "Like the A-Team."

Dan looked like he was about to fire back one of his very Danlike replies, but he was cut short by the loud hiss of the laboratory door and the steel shutters slamming shut over the window into the observation room.

"Containment Procedure Omega initiated," a robotic and slightly British voice announced over the loudspeaker. Why were ominous computer voices always British? "One minute to complete sterilization."

"Oh, man," Dan groaned. "What is complete sterilization?"

Dr. Miller's face drained of color. "It means the lab is going to be superheated to six hundred fifty degrees Fahrenheit to destroy any living cells inside it." He dropped one more syringe into the cooler. "Including us."

They had enough of the cure for two dozen people, and from that, they could grow more once they got to the surface. The cells reproduced quickly. They might have enough to save everyone.

Unless everything got burned to a crisp.

Dr. Miller snapped the case shut and hoisted it onto his shoulder. "We need to get out of here in the next minute," he said.

"Fifty-six seconds, actually," Sinead replied, already moving around the lab.

Dr. Miller was a biologist and Dan was a sarcastic fourteen-year-old daredevil with a merciless memory, but she knew chemistry. She'd finished all of high school chemistry when she was still in middle school and already had enough credits for a master's degree, if she had actually gone to college instead of going into hiding. It was amazing, the classes you could take on the Internet.

She rummaged through cabinets, looking for useful chemicals, and began mixing them at a furious pace. The countdown clock on the wall monitor showed her that thirty seconds had passed.

Thirty more to go.

Her hands shook as she pulled out the little liquid hydrogen container. She breathed to steady them. If she dropped her chemicals too soon, they wouldn't need the thirty seconds they had left. They'd be blown up before the lab incinerated itself.

She mixed a few more dribs and drabs of things no one in their right mind would ever want mixed, and then she had two sealed beakers ready to go.

She set them up against the steel shutter that blocked the observation room window.

"Step back," she warned, and they all pressed themselves against the opposite wall, ducking behind a heavy refrigerator unit. "Keep the vials safe."

Dr. Miller hugged them close.

Sinead aimed the air rifle at the window and fired. The shot hit the glass beakers, shattering one into the other, and the moment their contents mixed there was a puff of smoke, then a bubbling sound as they reacted to the air around them.

Dan wrinkled his brow. "What's supposed to happ—"

His question was cut short by the BOOM!

The explosion tore a hole in the steel shutter and shattered the thick glass behind it.

"Go!" Sinead yelled, shoving Dan toward the opening. He climbed through and then Dr. Miller passed him the cooler filled with the cure. He turned to Sinead and grabbed her by her suit, pushing her toward the hole.

"Go first!" he yelled.

"What are you doing?" she replied.

"No time!" the doctor yelled back. "I made this virus. You need to unmake it for me."

The clock on the wall showed three seconds as Dr. Miller shoved her through the opening. She stumbled and fell, rolling into the observation room just in time to see him press his back to the hole, blocking it off.

The monitors in the observation room displayed the countdown.

One second. Zero.

The back of Dr. Miller's suit sizzled and burst into blue flames, but his body had blocked the hole and saved them. The last words they heard him say over the radio in his headset as the heat burned him away were "I hear such beautiful music."

"No!" Sinead yelled. That should have been her in there. She was responsible. He'd invented the disease, but she'd unleashed it. How many lives had her choices cost? How many more would die because of her?

None, she decided. Whatever she had to do, she would get this cure to the surface.

"Come on!" Dan yelled, though his voice was hoarse with tears.

As they raced into the hall, the man with the Uzi opened fire, and Sinead shoved Dan to the floor.

The shots dented the wall behind them, but Sinead had her air rifle up to return fire.

Although *fire* was a strange word for it.

The gun made a hissing sound when it shot, and the blast was invisible. The only way she knew she'd hit her target was that the man went flying backward ten feet through the air, losing his weapon in the process.

Dan and Sinead popped to their feet and ran, side by side, for the hangar.

"We need to get the others and get out of here," Dan said.

"There's a submarine bay nearby," Sinead told him. "But Ian's weak and the others are still dancing . . . how will we move them?"

"Easy," Dan told her with that casual grin of his that she had to admit could be charming, when he wasn't using it to shred her pride. "We're going to fly there," he said.

CHAPTER 32

"This is crazy!" Nellie objected as Dan settled into the pilot's seat.

She rubbed her arm where Sinead had injected her with the cure.

"You think flying a private jet through the corridors of an undersea base below the Bermuda Triangle is crazy?" Dan asked. "Because I think it's totally awesome!"

That was Dan for as long as she'd known him, always aiming for the *totally awesome*, when *unreasonably dangerous* was the phrase Nellie would have chosen.

Nellie stood behind him, doing the shimmy as the cure worked its way into her system. She wasn't quite ready to sit down yet. Every time she made herself stop moving, she felt like her heart was trying to race out of her chest.

"Just be sure you can talk me through it, okay?" Dan said over his shoulder.

"I can," she assured him. She even patted him on the back, which he took as a gesture of comfort, but which she was really doing to drum the rhythm out of her arms. She had to keep drumming.

"Okay," she told him. "First, let's get that engine started up."

She guided Dan through the preflight sequence as best she could, and as the engine whined, then roared to life, he released the air brake and began to turn the plane toward the wide corridor out of the hangar.

Sinead had gone to the back with Amy, helping to inject the others with the cure and then get them secured. Dan had a red welt on his own neck and Nellie wanted to ask him what had happened, but she was also pretty sure she didn't want to know. Dan was okay right now, and that was all that mattered.

"If the hallways between here and the submarine docking bay narrow, we'll lose our wings," she told him.

"Good thing we won't have to fly for long, then, huh?" Dan put on the pilot's headset and spoke to the back of the plane. "Welcome to Dan Airlines. This is your captain speaking. Just wanted to let you fine folks know that it's going to be a bumpy ride."

"Maybe now's not the time for humor?" Nellie suggested.

"If not now," Dan replied, "when?"

He pointed the nose of the plane for the hangar opening just as the woman in the tracksuit came running in, armed. The man hobbled in after her, cradling his Uzi. They took aim and opened fire. Bullets tore into the windshield, making Dan and Nellie duck. Bullets sparked off the wings.

Dan pulled back the throttle, accelerating straight for their attackers. They kept firing and the bullets streaked past the plane and ricocheted off the side walls of the hangar.

A jet of water erupted from one little bullet hole in the base's hull.

Another bullet hit the wall.

Another jet of water sprayed out.

"Those lunatics are going to flood this base!" Nellie shouted.

"Well, let's make sure they're the only ones here when it happens!" Dan replied.

As he drove the plane straight at the shooters, forcing them to dive out of the way, she saw a slight grin flicker across his face. It made Nellie wince.

Dan was enjoying this.

She was doing the best she could to raise these kiddos, and after all they'd lost and all they'd suffered, it was a wonder they weren't both total psychopaths . . . but still . . . she wanted to preserve Dan's tenderness, not see it destroyed in a hail of gunfire or a ferocious flood.

All that, however, was a problem for later. The immediate problem occurred when there was a terrible jolt and a ferocious screech of metal tearing from metal. The plane veered hard to the right and the nose fell forward.

"They shot out one of our landing gear struts!" Amy yelled from the cabin.

Dan had to accelerate on one wheel and Nellie helped him pull back and aim straight through the wide hangar bay doors. Their wingtips sparked off the side with a sickening scrape.

"You need more speed!" she told him. He increased the throttle and she adjusted the flaps for him. As he pulled back, they had liftoff. It was only about an inch off the floor, but it worked.

"Looks like we're flying," Dan said. His knees bounced with adrenaline.

Dan had to keep the plane centered in the hallway, because they only had about a finger's length from each wingtip to the wall on either side, and not a long finger at that.

"You're doing great," Nellie gave him some encouragement. His hours of video-game playing were paying off. "Just, uh, watch out for the turn up ahead."

They were fast approaching a hard right turn, and there was no way the hall was wide enough for them to make it. They heard the rapid *rat tat tat* of gunfire on their tail. The ShkrellX goons were in pursuit, and they were all out of flying room.

They couldn't carry the sick fast enough to escape on foot. They'd be gunned down and left for dead at the bottom of the sea below the Bermuda Triangle, while above, the virus spread and ShkrellX charged billions of dollars for the cure.

"We're out of space!" Nellie yelled.

"Hang on," Dan told her. "It's going to be rough."

He sped up and lifted the nose of the plane. A trail of sparks rained down behind them as the tail scraped against the floor. Then Dan tilted, pitching the plane to the side, so the right wing dipped while the left wing thrust up to the ceiling.

Nellie almost fell, but she hung on to the back of the pilot's seat.

The right wing hit the floor and burst into bright orange flames, but it acted like the down-thrust arm of a runner pivoting around a tight turn. It spun them around the corner.

Of course, at the same time, the left wing tore a massive gash in the ceiling, through which water began to pour, and as they spun, both wings sheared off the sides of Jonah's once-luxurious jet.

The tube of the passenger cabin flew forward.

Severed from its wings, engines, and tail, and having no ability to fly, it hurtled down the corridor like a spear launched in battle. Then it hit the deck, rattling them all roughly, bounced, hit again, and slid—a steel and fiberglass stone skipped across a titanium lake.

Dan still held the controls, although there was nothing left for them to control. The back of the plane had torn off, and a wall of flaming wreckage blocked off the corridor behind them, with water flooding in to douse the flames.

Dan had bought them some time.

"That was terrible flying," Nellie told him. "But quick thinking."

He smiled. It was amazing that after all he'd been through, he still wanted to make Nellie proud. He had no idea, of course, how proud she was. She was in awe of him.

As soon as they slid to a stop, Dan was on his feet, rushing back into the cabin to make sure everyone was okay. Nellie followed.

Amy looked a bit worse for wear, but she was on her feet, checking on the sick passengers. None of them were squirming anymore. Nellie noticed that she, too, had stopped dancing, and it didn't hurt. She felt weird and tingly and tired, but . . . she was still. She was calm.

The relief that washed over her was profound. She grabbed Dan and hugged him.

"Hey!" Dan objected, as she knew he would, but didn't push her away.

The cabin was a mess of open bins, dropped oxygen masks, and torn wiring. At least with the tail ripped off, the stench wasn't so overpowering.

Saladin had discovered the busted-open cooler of snapper and was gleefully munching away. Nellie felt like her stomach was in her throat and, for the first time in her life, the look of a delicate pile of high-quality fish made her queasy.

She turned away.

"Can anybody walk?" she asked.

Ham began to unstrap himself from his seat, but as soon as he did, he slumped forward, too weak to stand. Jonah couldn't even get his seat belt off. Cara, however, stood on shaking legs and helped Jonah unbuckle. Sinead did her best to help Ham up. He looked to have lost a lot of weight, but he was still a big guy, and it could not have been easy for her to wrap his arm around her shoulder and hoist him.

"Good to see you again, Starling." He smiled at her. "Lift with your knees."

Ian stood up without help. His lips were profoundly chapped and his eyes were sunk deep in his head, but he opened his mouth and his voice creaked out, "Let's get off this wretched plane."

Amy helped him down, Sinead and Ham following, with Dan helping Jonah, Cara on her own, and Nellie and Saladin bringing up the rear. Nellie had the cooler with the last vials of the dancing virus cure over her shoulder. It was eerie holding the fate of all Havana and maybe all human civilization on her shoulder.

In a shuffling single file, they left the wreckage behind and made their way to the submarine bay door.

When they arrived, there was a man standing guard, one of the ShkrellX thugs, but he didn't even see them, although they walked right up to him.

He was dancing wildly.

Nellie reached for a syringe of the cure to give him, but Dan stopped her.

"We have to save it," he said. "For the innocents in Cuba. We don't have a lot left, and this guy chose his fate. He's with them."

"But, Dan—" Nellie objected, although Dan had already gone to help the others onto the submarine.

Nellie's heart sank. Was this the same Dan Cahill who used to collect baseball cards and tombstone rubbings? Was that boy lost forever to the man he was becoming far too young?

Once Dan was on board the sub, she injected the dancing guard with a syringe of the cure anyway. Nellie wouldn't let the brutality of the Cahills' enemies turn them brutal, too. Let Dan and Amy save the world. It was still Nellie's job to save *them*, even from themselves.

CHAPTER 33

Driving a submarine, it turned out, was just like riding a bike: They were both things that Amy had no idea how to do.

She was expert in a lot of things, things most seventeen-year-olds couldn't dream of, but neither riding a bike nor steering a small escape submarine was in her skill set. Of course, when riding a bike, if you fell off you probably just skinned your knee. You weren't several hundred feet below the surface of the ocean.

"Aim up," Dan advised her, and it was as good advice as any. She figured out that the thrusters guided her, while the angle of the sub's nose and flaps aimed her up or down. She aimed up and they rose away from the Ekat base as quickly as they could go.

"Do you think the ShkrellX people will make it out?" Nellie asked. Amy hadn't considered that. They'd not only intended to kill her and her brother, but also planned to murder millions of people in their profit-making scheme. Why should she care if they lived or died?

But of course, she did. She couldn't help it. She wanted them to face justice, not explode at the bottom of the sea.

"Oh, they made it," Dan said. "Unfortunately."

He tapped the sonar screen, and sure enough, there was another blip pulling away from the Ekat base.

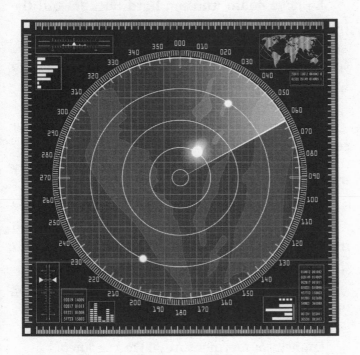

"They're coming after us," he added.

Dan was right. The other sub was closing in on them, and whoever was driving actually knew what they were doing.

Amy turned hard to port, then starboard again, zigzagging to lose the other sub. But it was a faster machine, and every zig she zigged or zag she zagged slowed them down more, while their pursuer sped up.

Amy couldn't lose them heading for the surface. They knew that was where she was going and they were on a course to cut her off.

So she aimed somewhere else.

She dove again, turning hard back toward the flooding Ekat base.

"Uh, Amy," Dan said. "I don't mean to back-seat drive, but you are kinda headed the wrong way."

"But so are they," she said.

An alarm blared and a red light on the computer console popped up.

"Projectile alert," the polite and, as usual, slightly British computer voice said.

"Pretty sure that's a torpedo," Dan said.

On the sonar screen, the small object launched from the other sub was cutting the distance toward them fast.

Beep. Beep. Beep, the sonar pinged, such an annoying sound to signal such a deadly turn of events.

Amy had no idea what to do.

"Launch countermeasures!" Dan shouted.

"What?" Amy didn't know what Dan was talking about.

"That's what they say in movies," Dan explained. "Just hit some buttons!"

Dan started hitting buttons on the console at random. Lights in the cockpit went on and off; the dash cam took a photo of an alarmed deepwater fish swimming below them, a big silver one with jagged teeth. They rolled side to side wildly in the water.

Whatever countermeasures were, Dan hadn't launched them.

"Stop it!" Amy yelled, swatting her little brother away and steadying the submarine.

Beep beep beep.

The missile closed in.

The fish below them was now alongside them.

"Any other great ideas?" Amy asked.

Dan's finger shot out and hit one more button, but all it did was unleash a prod from the side of the sub that sent a shock through the fish.

"Really helpful," Amy said.

"Impact in five seconds," the computer said. "Four. Three. Two—"

The fish bolted off, swimming away as fast as it could.

The torpedo was almost on them.

Beepbeepbeep. Beepbeepbeep. Beepbeepbeep.

"One," said the computer.

A BOOM shook the sub and sent them rolling forward, tail over head.

When they settled again, the torpedo was gone. No beeps.

"What just happened?" Nellie wondered.

Amy studied the sonar screen, brow furrowed. She looked at Dan. They both had the same realization, but Dan spoke it aloud first.

"They torpedoed the fish."

Nellie looked horrified, but Amy and Dan burst out laughing.

A smile still on her face, Amy reset her course back down toward the base.

As the large undersea structure loomed into view, she saw how a few sectors of it had already lost power, their lights shut off as it flooded section by section.

The other submarine hailed them on the radio. They were closing in fast.

"Cahills, this is Jonathan West," he said. "You have stolen my property. Surrender now, let me board, and I will allow you to live."

"No thanks," Amy replied.

"Then I will blow you out of the water!" he answered.

"You blow us up," Amy said, "and you destroy the cure, too. Dr. Miller died. There's no one left to rediscover it."

Mr. West didn't answer. Or rather, his answer came in the form of another blip on the sonar.

"Projectile alert," the annoying British computer voice warned again.

"Incoming!" Mr. West cackled over the radio.

"He's gone nuts," Dan said.

This time Amy had a plan. "Everyone else strapped in?" she asked.

"Affirmative," Sinead said.

"This is not a way to travel in style," Ian said. "But we are secure."

"Uggh, my head," Hamilton groaned, finally regaining the power of speech and, with it, the rest of his senses. He had a giant bump where he'd been bashing Amy's biohazard suit. She felt bad for the guy. If he felt half as bad as he looked, he was in for a rough recovery.

But he had to be alive to recover, and that was up to Amy.

She aimed the sub at one of the big air-scrubbing tanks on the perimeter of the base and slowed down.

"Impact in five seconds," the computer said. "Four. Three. Two—"

Beepbeepbeep. Beepbeepbeep. Beepbeepbeep.

"Amy," Ian's voice called from the rear of the sub. "I don't mean to be a bother, but . . ."

"Hang on!" Amy revved the throttle and pulled up just before they hit the air tank. The bottom of their sub scraped against it, letting out a thin stream of bubbles from the narrow gash they made.

The torpedo on their tail couldn't bend up in time. It smashed into the air tank, punching a hole straight into it.

"One," said the computer voice.

There was a boom; their submarine shuddered again as they were consumed by the roar of escaping air from the exploding tank.

But the air provided a cushion against the blast. The rush of rising bubbles hid their sub like a smoke screen, and the debris from the broken tank rose alongside them as Amy aimed up and tried to hold their rise steady. There was no way for Mr. West's sonar to tell that they were in there.

As far as he knew, he'd blown them up.

"Not bad for your first submarine chase," Nellie told Amy, and she smiled. An exploded fish, a destroyed air tank on a flooded base, a fake sub explosion . . . maybe it wasn't bad for her first time, but it wasn't so good, either.

She decided she'd finally learn to ride a bike when they got back to Attleboro. She had no desire to drive a submarine again.

But first, they had to get the cure to Dr. Neuman in Havana. They had to begin growing more of it in his lab right away. There were a lot of doomed dancers counting on it. The sub made amazing speed for Cuba, and Amy prayed there would still be anyone left to save when they got there.

CHAPTER 34

Havana, Cuba

One by one, the dancers stopped dancing.

They gave the cure they had to the most serious cases first. A girl on life support. A boy who looked more like a skeleton than a human being. All the drummers Sinead had infected.

Then they were forced to wait. As the dancers healed, nurses drew their blood and used it to create more of the cure for the dancing virus, and gave it to more of the victims. The more people they cured, the more people they could cure.

In a few hours, they were well on their way to curing everyone. By the next afternoon, the infected were all getting rehydrated and resting.

"I am proud to say," Dr. Neuman boasted, "we have zero fatalities on the island. Thanks to Dr. Miller's sacrifice, what could have killed millions, killed no one."

"Oh, thank you!" Sinead burst into tears and hugged the doctor. Dan wondered what she was so relieved about. Sure, her attempt to cure an outbreak she'd caused succeeded, but that didn't mean she was innocent. He still hadn't quite decided what to do about her.

Outside of the hospital, they all gathered to pile into the giant Packard that Ned was driving.

"Headache free," Ned said. "Turns out a little Caribbean vacation was just what I needed."

Beside him, Ted and Flamsteed sat in the front seat. The service dog was wearing his own guayabera shirt to match his master's.

"They found a pet store," Ned explained. "Turns out the people of Havana pamper their dogs as much as the people of Boston do."

"Looks like you guys had a good time without us," Dan said. Ted and Ned weren't the type to let a dangerous disease dampen their spirits.

"I might have liked to enjoy some of the famous music while I was here," Ted told him. "But because of the outbreak, they shut down all the nightclubs."

"We actually have to send police out tonight," Dr. Neuman said. "To tell people it's safe to dance again. I bet the music will begin before even the first officer arrives. Word travels fast in Havana. Nothing stays secret for long."

"I think that's why we better get going," Amy suggested. "We did sneak back in on a submarine."

Dr. Neuman laughed. "I have spoken to our Presidente Castro. The Cahills are welcome to come and go from Cuba any time."

"Even though we're loyal to your enemy nation?" Dan asked, eyebrows raised.

"The United States is not our enemy," Dr. Neuman said, grinning. "Besides, the Cahills are citizens of the world. You belong to no nation."

"Like the A-Team!" Nellie clapped.

Dan frowned.

"There is one favor our leader asked of you before he can allow you to leave." Dr. Neuman took a deep breath. His face looked pained as he prepared to ask his question. He turned away from Dan and looked at Jonah. "The Castro brothers are big fans of your work, Jonah Wizard. They would like an autograph."

He thrust an old press photo of Jonah into the teen pop star's face, and Ham had to react quickly to intercept it.

"No autographs," he grumbled in his best body-guard voice. He still looked sickly and pale, so the effect was not nearly as intimidating as Ham was trying to make it.

"It's cool," Jonah said, taking the photo and a pen and inscribing the picture *To Raúl and Fidel: Keep it Real, Bros. Peace.*

"You know they're vicious dictators?" Amy whispered to Jonah.

He just shrugged. "That's why I wrote *peace*. Pop culture diplomacy. Like when David Bowie played at the Berlin Wall in 1987."

"You are *not* David Bowie," Ham told him firmly, and the two began to argue about musical legacies and performance art.

Dan, who could not have been less interested, went to pet Saladin in his cat carrier on the backseat. As he bent down, two shadows fell across his face. He looked up through the window opposite and saw two dark ties against white dress shirts in dark suits. He stood up to peer over the roof of the car on his tiptoes and saw two faces wearing dark sunglasses.

"Agent Gimler, Agent Pratt," he said. "Nice to see you."

They frowned in unison. "Who?"

"I'm just a traveling saxophonist. Named Gimler," said Agent Gimler.

"And I'm a guitar player. Named Pratt," said Agent Pratt.

Both agents cast obviously fake smiles at Dr. Neuman.

"Our band is called The Agents," said Agent Pratt. "That's what Dan meant."

Dr. Neuman rolled his eyes and returned to the hospital with his signed Jonah Wizard photo, muttering about the foolishness of the CIA.

Dan stood up straight as the poorly disguised CIA agents stepped around the car on either side of him.

"You did well, Dan Cahill," Agent Gimler said.

"A great service to your country," Agent Pratt added. "We even arrested a Mr. Jonathan West, whose submarine surfaced a few miles off of Bermuda. Turns out, his own company wanted him arrested for diverting millions of dollars to a research project they now deny all knowledge of. Looks like he'll be going to jail."

"But your work is not yet done," Agent Gimler said, then he turned to Sinead. "Sinead Starling, you need to come with us."

"Where are you taking her?" Amy asked.

"That is not of your concern, Amy," said Agent Pratt. "You did your job, finding her and isolating this outbreak. We'll need to collect samples of this disease to secure at USAMRIID, and Ms. Starling needs to be debriefed."

"Debriefed," Ian scoffed. "I believe that is one of your quaint American spy ways of describing torture." He gave Sinead a look that could have sliced concrete. "Not that I mind, of course."

Sinead stiffened. Her eyes darted left and right, and Dan knew she was thinking of running. He also knew she wouldn't get far on her own. She'd committed serious crimes and put the entire world in danger.

Dan looked over at Amy, who was looking at Nellie. Nellie was looking at Dan, looking at him like she was afraid of him, afraid of what he might do.

But Sinead deserved what she had coming, didn't she?

Ham and Jonah had barely survived the disease they'd caught in her lab. Ian had been practically dead already when Amy got to him, and Cara wouldn't have been far behind. Dan was next if he hadn't gotten the cure, and so was Nellie. How did they expect him to forgive Sinead for all that?

She admitted that she'd stolen the disease and unleashed it to save her own skin. She was guilty. She'd even admitted she was guilty.

Then again, none of them were exactly innocent. Ham had set the bomb that injured Sinead's brothers. Jonah had actually killed someone. Ian had been merciless with his own enemies—including at one time Amy and Dan—and Cara had helped her father nearly take over the world. If everyone got what they deserved, what hope was there for any of them?

Everyone made mistakes. Everyone acted selfishly sometimes and made bad choices, and everybody hurt someone else at some point, whether they meant to or not. Everyone had regrets.

Leadership wasn't about having a perfect memory for every right and wrong; it was learning when to forget and when to forgive. There was an old saying, that holding a grudge was like drinking poison and waiting for your enemy to die from it.

Dan had held enough grudges. He looked at Sinead and then back to the agents.

"We've got a problem," he told them. "The virus has been eliminated. Whatever was in that hospital, Dr. Neuman has already incinerated down to the last molecule, and whatever was in the Bermuda Triangle—well, it's as gone as anything that ever went down there. I don't think anybody, even the US government, should have samples of this virus in their lab. There's no reason. Its only use is as a weapon. So it's gone. Let it go. And as for Sinead

Starling . . . well . . ." He looked at her again. He made his choice. No more poison. It was time to forgive her. "She's one of us, and she stays with us."

Out of the corner of Dan's eye, he saw Nellie smile. Amy, too.

They didn't stay smiling for long, though. Nellie's face bent into a frown, and Amy's eyes widened.

He followed his sister's gaze down to Agent Gimler's hand, where he'd drawn a gun and pointed it at Dan.

"Oh man!" Dan groaned. "Again with this?"

CHAPTER 35

"If you want Sinead Starling, the traitor, that badly," said Agent Gimler, "then you can have her. But there are samples of the virus for us to take, and we are taking them."

"I told you," Dan replied. "There aren't. We destroyed all of it."

"And Dr. Miller died," Sinead added. "There's no way for anybody to make more. Only he knew how. I think that's why he sacrificed himself, so that no one could ever learn his deadly recipe."

"See?" said Amy. "All gone."

"No," said Agent Pratt, as he and Agent Gimler moved closer to the open car door where Dan was standing. "There is still one living sample of the virus."

The agent's eyes went to the cat carrier on the backseat.

Of course, Amy thought. Saladin had been given the virus. It couldn't hurt him, but he carried it inside him, along with the basic ingredients of the cure. He was like a walking, napping, purring biological weapon.

There was no way Amy was going to let these agents take him.

Saladin meowed when all eyes went to him, no doubt thinking he was about to be let out of the very undignified crate and served a late lunch. He coughed an impatient hairball.

"You can't take our cat," Dan said, moving to block the open car door with his body, just as Agent Gimler moved to grab the cat carrier. Agent Pratt rushed Dan from behind.

"Get your hands off my brother!" Amy yelled, channeling all her rage and exhaustion into a hard kick at the back of Agent Pratt's knee.

"Ahh!" His leg buckled and he fell.

Amy spun, delivering a solid uppercut to the other agent's solar plexus, which doubled him over. She wrapped her fingers around his gun hand, trying to pry the pistol loose, as she shouted at Dan: "Run!"

Her brother grabbed the cat carrier and bolted. Agent Pratt stood up to chase him, but Hamilton and Sinead rushed him, tackling him backward through the passenger's side window of the Packard. He fell right onto Ted's lap, which prompted three quick barks from Flamsteed.

"I wouldn't move if I were you," warned Ted, and Agent Pratt lay there in his lap, his legs sticking out the window and dog drool sliding down his face.

Agent Gimler, however, wriggled free of Amy and ran after Dan.

She realized she had just attacked two US government agents while on the soil of another country. Did that make her a traitor? Or were they breaking the law by operating in Cuba at all? She couldn't imagine she was in the right, but she couldn't imagine they were, either, trying to steal some children's cat to run medical experiments on.

Maybe nobody was right and nobody was wrong, everybody just did their best in the space between, and if, at the end of the day, everybody got home safely, it was a win.

She just had to make sure they all *did* get home safely. She didn't want Dan to do anything crazy.

Amy sprinted after Agent Gimler, hoping to catch up before her brother committed treason against the US government. She noticed, with a glance to a nearby rooftop, that there were other agents pursuing Dan, too. Rooftop snipers. Agent Pratt and Agent Gimler were not alone.

She ran faster.

Agent Pratt had gotten away from Flamsteed out the opposite window and was running after her. The dog was barking at the backseat of the car instead of chasing Agent Pratt. Amy didn't have time to wonder why.

Dan whipped around the corner of a wide block and did an overly showy slide across the hood of a car. The driver honked and screamed at him in Spanish, blocking Agent Gimler's path for a moment, long enough that Amy could catch up.

"Just let my brother go!" she yelled. "You don't need this disease in your lab!"

The agent ignored her and kept going, so she sprinted after him. Just as she was about to trip him from behind, a piece of the wall beside her burst apart. She looked up and saw one of the snipers wag a finger of warning at her. He could have blown her head off from this distance, but he hadn't wanted to. He just wanted to back her off.

It worked.

She backed off.

But only until the sniper had moved on to continue chasing Dan. Once she saw he was gone, she kept pursuing Agent Gimler. They ran from the neighborhood of tall buildings and grand boulevards built in the 1960s, back into the Old Havana neighborhood built during the eighteenth-century Spanish settlement. The streets here were narrow, winding, and filled with tourists. Which way would Dan have gone? If she lost him, would he try to fight off the CIA agents? Would they put a bullet in him to get their cat?

Amy picked a random direction. The streets wound and twisted. Booksellers lined the sidewalks, and crowded outdoor cafés bustled. Buskers with guitars entertained the tourists. As she ran past, every café had a different musician out front playing for tips, so that her chase sounded a bit like flipping stations on the radio. She heard countless snippets of the famous tune "*Guantanamera.*"

She crossed through a great square ringed by iron balconies on pink stone buildings. An old baroque cathedral stood sentinel and Amy would have loved to take some time to explore it, to learn about its history, but instead, she ran past it, down a side street, past the stenciled logo of the CDR, the ominous eye and sword, and then ran out into a narrow park.

On the other side of the park, there was a wide, fast-moving road, and her brother was moving across it, one lane at a time, waiting and bolting as cars and trunks honked and shouted.

Beyond the road, her brother ran for the seawall that dropped into the water of Havana Bay. Agent Gimler followed, and a glance at the rooftop showed Amy not one, but two snipers taking positions across the park. They had pretty clear views of her brother as he held Saladin's cat carrier over the fence and threatened to drop it if Agent Gimler took another step closer.

Amy took a deep breath and braved the road crossing herself, coming up behind Agent Gimler just as the CIA operative raised his empty hands and told Dan to stay calm. Agent Pratt kept his distance on the other side of the road. He was catching his breath with his head between his knees.

"Tell your snipers to stand down!" Dan yelled, still threatening to toss Saladin's crate over the edge.

"Okay, okay . . ." Agent Gimler said, then whispered an order into the microphone on his collar.

"They're standing down. Just don't do anything crazy."

"Crazy?" Dan roared. "You manufacture a deadly disease, let a teenager steal it, leave *other* teenagers to stop it from destroying the world, and then, when the only remaining sample of the virus is in their pet cat, you threaten to catnap him to make *more* of the virus?! *That's* crazy. What I'm doing now, it's the *only* sane thing left!"

"Dan?" Amy asked calmly. "What *are* you doing now?"

"Saladin's the only way they can make more of this disease," Dan said. "We can't let them. It nearly killed Ian, and Ham, and Jonah, and Cara. Even Nellie. It could've killed me, too. All of us. It can't be allowed to exist. I won't let it! I won't!"

Dan's cheeks flushed red, and his lip quivered. He was fighting back tears.

He hefted the crate farther over the edge.

"I'm sorry," Dan said to her, and then turned to the cat carrier. "I'm so sorry." His voice cracked. He couldn't fight back the tears any longer, and he wept, hot tears pouring down his cheeks, snot bursting from his nose with heaving, anguished gasping breaths and then, with a cry of rage and pain that could have made the statues on the great cathedral of Havana weep, he hurled Saladin's crate into the crashing waves below.

"No!" Agent Gimler yelled.

The agent and Amy rushed to the edge in unison, looking down as the crate bobbed once, twice, then smashed against the rocks and sank below the waves.

Dan whimpered, and Amy put her arm around him. His whole body was shaking. She'd never seen him show this much emotion. It was like every sob he'd never allowed himself to sob before had burst from him at once.

Agent Gimler looked at him with a mix of horror, rage, and a small amount of regret.

"We did the job you hired us to do," said Amy. "Our business is done. If we have any more trouble, the *Boston Globe*, the *New York Times*, the *Washington Post*, and *Buzzfeed* will all hear about the government's illegal virus experiments and how the CIA made two orphaned children murder their own cat."

"But—you—I can't believe he just—" Agent Gimler stammered.

"I did what needed to be done," said Dan, straightening his back and wiping his nose on his sleeve. "That's what Cahills do."

A group of men under one of the CDR logos had taken an interest in the scene, and one of them was walking toward a police car to report the suspicious activity. Agent Gimler muttered under his breath, then ordered his team to pull out. It wouldn't do to have US government agents caught operating in Havana. The Cubans had their own way of "debriefing" prisoners.

Agent Gimler sighed. "Thanks for saving the world, anyway," he grumbled. "Sorry about your cat." He shook his head and left them by the water's edge.

Amy could feel Dan still shuddering beneath his T-shirt, and she held him tighter as they walked away in the other direction, back into the winding streets of Old Havana, to collect their friends and make their way, at last, for home.

CHAPTER 36

Attleboro, Massachusetts

They lay in streaks of sunlight, moving their chairs to track the luminescent paths across the room as the day went by. They took all the good spots.

None of them spoke much, tired as they were, their bodies healing. He could smell the sickness leaving them, health and vigor returning to each one as the days passed.

The big blond boy, Hamilton, watched rugby matches on television and talked endlessly about some sort of sports league he planned to join so he could "crack skulls and find a date," while the one who was always singing, Jonah, watched videos of himself on the Internet, shuddering with every dance move he made. He swore he would never dance again, but none of the others believed him. Ian, as always clad in his finely tailored fabrics, read financial news all day, and Saladin did his best to scratch his pant legs to tatters. The fancier the fabric, the deeper the scratches.

It drove the boy mad, because he couldn't see the lesson that Saladin was trying to teach him, a lesson cats knew well: Everything can be damaged, but damage is not destruction. It is change. Though the process can be painful, everything changes.

Saladin had changed.

One moment, he was sitting in his cat carrier in the infernal heat of whatever city Dan and Amy's adventures had taken them to. He was well traveled, that he knew, more so than other cats. He was, however, quite tired of travel. At his age, travel was not a luxury so much as a burden. They'd hauled him all over the world for some time now.

He would bear his burden with as much good cheer as he could, which was to say, with no good cheer at all. Cats of his age did not *do* "good cheer."

They also did not do cat carriers. It was an insult to his dignity and also tended to make him airsick.

So, while Dan and Amy had discussed some business or other with those two agitated gentlemen in the dark suits, Saladin had slipped his claw through the back of the carrier and made his way out of the flap he used to escape, the flap that none of his humans seemed aware of.

Except, as he slid from the carrier to hide in the shade beneath the seat, he caught the eye of young Dan.

Dan, most puzzlingly, winked at him.

Saladin did not *do* winks, either.

He vanished underneath the seat, wondering what on earth Dan's wink could have meant, and also wondering how long he would have to wait for his next meal to be served. He did not intend to wait all day, and if they did not present him with his preferred fish soon, he would have to take his claws to one of their legs to teach them a lesson about patience and service.

His lack of patience, and *their* required service.

It struck him as odd, however, when Dan grabbed the now-empty cat carrier and ran away with it, the other humans—including Amy—giving chase. Why did Dan care so much for an empty cat carrier? He knew it was empty. Did he just enjoy a jog?

Humans were terribly odd creatures.

Odder still, some time later when they returned and those odd men in suits had all gone, Amy was weeping. She wept and wept, until finally, Dan reached under the seat and hauled Saladin into the bright and merciless sunlight.

Amy hugged Saladin so hard that he felt he might need to remind her he was not a dog, like that slobbering goon in the front seat, but he sighed and allowed her to stroke his fur. It felt nice, after all. He gave her a purr, to show he was not entirely unappreciative.

"You . . . you *faked* it?" Amy asked, a tone of almost feline incredulity in her voice.

Dan shrugged. "What? You thought I was a monster? I'd never kill our cat."

Give me lunch, then, Saladin thought at them, but his thoughts were not loud enough for humans to hear.

"I knew they'd never leave us alone as long as they thought Saladin was alive," Dan continued. "And all it cost us was a cat carrier."

"You nearly broke my heart," Amy said, and slugged Dan on the arm. "Next time give me a wink or something."

"I figured you knew," Dan said. "I thought I was overacting. You really thought I'd blow snot bubbles in public?"

After that odd experience and more conversation that did not end in Saladin getting his lunch, they flew home. They napped. They ate. The one in the fancy pants performed something called a "hostile takeover" of some company called ShkrellX Pharmaceuticals, announcing to the others that they now owned the company that had been the cause of all this trouble, and that shares were trading at above-average volume, whatever that meant. The one called Sinead would be allowed to work in research and development at the new company.

Business never interested Saladin much. Meals did.

They finally fed him until he had no desire to eat anymore.

Now, here he was, wandering the halls of the mansion, looking for a good patch of sun to lie in and finding all his favorite ones taken by these humans in their recovery.

Saladin had to find new patches to lie in for himself, if he didn't want to be petted whenever he lay down, but every time he came near one of the windows, Dan grabbed him and pulled him away, setting him back on the floor.

"Sorry, Saladin," he said. "You can't be seen. You're in hiding now. The authorities need to believe you died in Cuba."

Saladin coughed up a particularly nasty hairball, just to tell Dan how he felt about this new situation. No windows for Saladin? Did they not know this was his house long before it was theirs?

He knew himself to be carrying this strange disease they'd all been so worried about. He could feel it in his body, the way he could feel the weather changing or sense impending danger. Cat instincts. He couldn't understand how humans survived without them.

The disease didn't bother him the way it seemed to bother the rest of them when they were dancing around like maniacs for two days.

Now that they were better, he understood he was the only being alive who carried this virus inside him. Dan had explained that to the others, and Saladin had heard. He understood the humans far better than they knew. He always had. Humans were quite fascinating to watch when you paid attention.

Of course, he knew that this sickness was dangerous to them, fragile and furless as they were. He knew that he must be careful not to let it out.

He felt a little swell of feline pride at the idea. In him, flowing through his veins, was the power to save humanity or to destroy it. Just like it was with the rest of the Cahill family.

His family.